Merlin's Mound

Nigel Bryant's involvement with Arthurian matters is long-standing. As theatre director and radio drama producer he has worked on Arthur-related plays and series by writers including C.S.Lewis, Rosemary Sutcliff, Susan Cooper and Kevin Crossley-Holland, and as a translator he has published modern English versions of *The High Book of the Grail (Perlesvaus),* the *Perceval* of Chrétien de Troyes and its Continuations, Robert de Boron's *Merlin and the Grail* and a new compilation of the medieval French romances, *The Legend of the Grail.*

Cover:
photograph of Silbury Hill by Adam Dale,
(www.dalephotographics.co.uk); inset photograph of harvest goddess (the Harvest Home "Kern Baby" of 1901, Whalton, Northumberland) reproduced by kind permission of Birmingham Central Library (Benjamin Stone Collection Box 270/7); cover design by Jevan Bryant.

Merlin's Mound

Nigel Bryant

Published by
Mandrake of Oxford
PO Box 250
OXFORD
OX1 1AP (UK)

A CIP catalogue record of this book is available from the British
Library and the US Library of Congress.

ISBN 1869928-76-8

Printed and bound in Great Britain
by Antony Rowe Ltd, Chippenham

In memory of P.B.K.

Contents

Merlin's Mound

*T*he silence was broken by a tinkling of bells, and a figure came scrambling from beneath the king's table. He lurched towards Jo and the knights, clapping his hands and laughing inanely. He was babbling:

"Here he is! Here he is! A saviour at last! A saviour!"

And fixing his wondering gaze upon Jo, the Fool said softly:

"I tell you true: this boy could be the one! He's stupendous! He can see the past and see the gods. He's seen the Lady of the Lake!"

1. The Dig

He awoke with a start. The telephone was ringing, and he had, for a moment, no idea who he was.

For that brief, strange period of time he could, he felt, be anyone; he felt he could do anything.

But it didn't last. He was Jo. It was the middle of the afternoon. He'd fallen asleep in the hotel room and the 'phone needed answering. For what might have been a minute, but was probably no more than three telephone rings, he lay and let his eyes drift around the walls. They were painted the palest of English pinks – the colour of the roses in the little framed prints, chosen, he supposed, to appeal to the tourists who pitched up in this perfectly English town. He sniffed. The whole room reeked of air-freshener. The 'phone rang on. And then it dawned on him:

At last! At long last! It could be her!

He nearly fell off the bed in his scramble for the receiver. He picked it up.

"Mum?" he said, beaming.

And that was the moment when the strangeness *really* started. Because the sound that came through the ear-piece was unlike any telephone tone: it was the sound of deep water, or moving air.

"Mum?" he said again.

Was there anybody there at all?

"Mum?" he said a third time. "Is that you?"

And then, out of the wind and water, it seemed a voice was

12

taking shape; and it was neither old nor young, neither male nor female, and it said, with the utmost certainty:

"Jo. Here begin the terrors. Here begin the marvels."

* * *

"You're not eating your breakfast."

"No, Dad. Not at *this* time."

"Come on, Jo, come on. We've got to be at the dig by nine."

Jo propped a cheek on one hand and groped for a spoon with the other. "Why do we have to start so early?"

"Early? It's not early," said his father, frowning, desperate for him to get on. "In the real world this is when people start work. It's only you adolescents who think getting up at noon is normal. Oh for heaven's sake stop playing with that cereal and eat it."

"Okay, okay. Indigestion here I come." And Jo shovelled in two mounds of flakes, milk dribbling down his chin.

"What's up with you?" said his dad, glancing across the breakfast room, hoping no-one was watching. "Don't you like it here?"

" 'S allright."

"Most kids your age would think it was fantastic. Damn good hotel and an excavation."

"Yeah," said Jo. "They would."

His dad took a breath and ignored this. Then he said: "I reckon we're going to find something really special," and he stroked his neatly shaven chin. "The whole team thinks so. This could be the biggest event in British archaeology for decades! Headline news without a doubt - TV, the lot!"

Jo looked up to see his father's face aglow. He was performing for the cameras already, thought Jo. And he was saying:

"It's amazing the place has never been excavated before. Rich pickings!" His chair creaked as he rocked backwards. "And you could be there when I find them!"

Jo scraped the bowl and let his spoon drop with a clatter.

"Couldn't you, Jo?"

"Mmm?"

"Oh please!" said his dad, his chair thumping forward. "Do we have to have these teenage grunts?" He closed his eyes to contain his irritation. "I'm saying, you could be on hand at a major archaeological find. Aren't you excited? No other kid would have the chance."

"Yeah. Yeah, it's great." As Jo scratched his scalp and looked away, he caught sight of himself in a gold-framed mirror, and was surprised by his own height - and troubled by the bright red spot below his lip, and the way his hair stuck out over his ear: was it too long, or too short? It would never hang right. Nice shirt, though: his favourite shade of blue, and he specially liked the floppy, frayed collar and the -

"Jo! Jo, the waitress is asking you a question."

Jo looked round and said: "Mmm?"

* * *

It was an extraordinary site for a dig. They stood in a narrow tarmac pathway at the back of what Jo had been told was a famous public school. Behind them, a jumble of buildings: a Victorian brick structure, foursquare and imposing; the side of a Georgian mansion, with stately windows and an elegant door; and a concrete-and-glass job from the 1960s, complete with boilers, oil tanks, bikesheds and dustbins.

And in front of them, the looming, mighty Stone Age mound.

"Shame they had to plant trees all over it," said his father, looking up at the spindly trunks that sprouted from the mound in all directions. "They did that in the seventeenth century - and cut that naff spiral pathway to take 'em to the top. Look at it. A folly, I suppose they called it. Too true."

14

"What's wrong with it?" said Jo with a shrug. "It looks okay."

His father sighed in the sunshine. "You've got no idea," he murmured.

"What d'you mean?"

"In the Stone Age this would've been spectacular."

"Well it's still pretty big."

"Yes," said his father with a snort. "And how d'you think they made it? Oh do stop slouching, Jo."

Jo tutted and stood absurdly rigid, like a guardsman.

"Look, in a year or two you're going to be a strapping lad - make the most of yourself. Walk tall. You don't need a designer slouch like that whatshisname."

"Who?"

"That moronic footballer you go on about. And get your hair cut - but not like him."

Jo closed his eyes.

"I mean *they* couldn't do it," his dad said, and when Jo looked up, wondering what he meant, he saw him pointing at a builder's truck with three hunched smokers in the front seat, turning into the school grounds. "That lot wouldn't know where to start. Underneath all these weeds and trees," he said, shading his eyes from the sun as he gazed upwards, "this is a huge mound of chalk blocks - cut with picks made from antlers and spades from cattle's shoulder-blades! Incredible! Look at the size of it: must be sixty-odd feet, easy. And the base would fill most of Trafalgar Square! It's almost on the scale of the pyramids!"

"Yeah," Jo murmured. "What was the point?"

"Well, that's what we're about to find out!" His father rubbed his hands and smiled. Jo noticed how white his teeth were. "But it's obviously a burial mound, and judging by the size it was for someone pretty special. There's a four-and-a-half-thousand-year-old treasure under there - waiting for me to find it!"

"I thought you said it was Merlin," said Jo, kicking a stone into an imaginary goal.

"What?"

"I thought you said it was Merlin who was buried here."

"Oh, no," his father said, and batted away a fly. "That's just a story. The locals like to think it's where Marlborough got its name - Merlin's Barrow or some such nonsense. They've even got it on the town's motto: UBI NUNC SAPIENTIS OSSA MERLINI."

"Do what?"

His father gave a huffing laugh, and muttered: "What *do* they teach you these days?" Then he said: "It means: WHERE NOW ARE THE BONES OF WISE MERLIN."

"Wow," said Jo, almost interested.

"It's not wow at all, it's rubbish. This mound's the same age as Silbury Hill -"

"Oh yeah? What's that?"

" - an even bigger mound up the road there near Avebury, and that's two and a half thousand BC which is a damn sight earlier than King Arthur stories."

"And what have they found under Silbury Hill?"

"Well...nothing," said his dad. "It's completely empty. But it doesn't mean this one will be. I can't wait. Let's go!"

* * *

The dig had been going on for hours, and to Jo's inexperienced eye they had achieved next to nothing. A pile of *carefully* banked chalk and soil; roots and plant matter *carefully* sifted; and a tiny collection of *carefully* brushed objects of absolutely zero interest as far as Jo could see. For some reason, grown men and women who should have known better were showing serious excitement about a small section of antler.

"What a start!" said his father, cradling it in his hand. "Think, Jo: this is one of the tools used to dig the mound. Four and a half thousand years ago, a Stone Age fist gripped this and hacked away at the chalk."

Jo had a look and said: "Mmm."

They were beginning the dig by burrowing a tunnel more or less horizontally from the middle of one side of the mound, aiming for a point in the exact centre.

"That's where the treasure'll be, obviously," said Jo's father. "And if it's not, we'll dig a vertical shaft down to the base in case it's right at the bottom."

His father's enthusiasm, the adrenalin pumping through his veins and voice, made Jo all the more sober, all the more determined to be cynical.

"How many years are you planning to be here?" he said, slumping into a canvas chair. "At the rate you've been going this morning it'll be - "

"Damn it, I knew you'd be like this!" his father snapped. "I've told you before, archaeology is painstaking work. You don't just call in a JCB and gouge a damn great hole through the place."

"I bet you would if you had to."

"What?"

"Well you would, wouldn't you?" Jo said, and leaned back in the chair, hands behind head. "You don't care about this place. That tunnel you're digging's hideous. You're ruining it already."

His father stood and looked at Jo with utter disdain. "Everything's being properly logged and recorded," he said coolly. "The whole site will be respected."

"Respected?" Jo raised his eyebrows dramatically.

"Of course. There's probably a great king buried under here. We're disturbing his grave. How would you feel if someone dug into *your* grave in a thousand years' time?"

"Exactly!" said Jo, and pushed himself out of the chair, irritated and uncomfortable. He was struggling to see his father's logic; and then something else dawned on him. He turned to his dad and stood up tall and said: "I didn't think they had kings in those times."

"What?"

"In the days when Stonehenge and Avebury were built, I didn't think they had kings."

"What do *you* know about it?"

"I've read it in your own books." Jo glowed: he felt as if he'd trumped an ace.

His father shifted uneasily, and smoothed his black and thinning hair. "Well - not *kings* exactly, no. I was just trying to put it in words you'd understand. Let's face it, it's got to be someone pretty important if they built a mound this size."

"If it's a burial mound at all."

"What?" his father said with a lop-sided grin of ridicule. "What else could it be?"

"I don't know, really." Jo was suddenly distant; he looked idly up at the mound's great bulk. "It just doesn't feel right."

"What are you talking about, Jo?"

Jo shrugged.

"Well?"

He shrugged again.

"Oh, very eloquent," his father said, snatching up a trowel. "Very articulate. One step down from the teenage grunt. If you don't want to watch what we're doing, go and find something more interesting to do."

"What," said Jo with a laugh, "in Marlborough?"

"Why not?"

"There's nothing here. Hasn't even got a cinema."

"That's about the size of it, isn't it?" said his father, with a single, angry stride towards him. "If you were back at home you'd be glued to the box or those bloody computer games. Unless you've got a screen in front of you, you're... Or a football - oh yes, mustn't forget the football. Life stops for that, of course, but otherwise you're completely - "

"Oh, shut up, Dad!" Suddenly Jo was furious. "I told you I didn't want to come down to your boring dig in boring Wiltshire. Interfering with some burial. If there *is* someone down there,

18

maybe you should leave him be."

"Don't talk such utter - "

"Well? What right have you got to dig into a grave?"

His father laughed at this absurd question. "It's archaeological research!"

"So?"

His dad thought he hadn't heard him. He said again, louder: "It's archaeological research."

"I know," said Jo, simply. "So?"

There was a moment's silence as father and son stood staring at each other. Then:

"Well," the father said at last... and then paused, completely wrong-footed by the one-syllable question. "...Well...it's important work: we're expanding our knowledge of the past."

"And this is the only way of doing it, is it?" said Jo. "Vandalising mounds?"

"What *are* you talking about?" His father was all the more aggressive for having been unsettled. "Eh?"

Jo was curiously unsettled himself. "I don't know, really."

"You're telling me."

"I just feel..."

Jo stopped. He had brushed back his hair and was gazing up towards the tree-covered summit of the mound, silent and huge in the dusty sunshine. He had no idea why, but he was beginning to sense that it was a quite extraordinary place.

"What?" said his father, irritation now uncontained; and with the utmost contempt for the word, he said: "What is it you *'feel'*?"

"I don't know," Jo said softly. "I just feel there must be another way of seeing it."

"Seeing what?"

"The past."

2. The Grotto

*T*he August sun beat down. There was only the slightest breeze. It was a beautiful day, and there was nothing to do. To Jo, the archaeologists' work was mind-numbing, so he wandered off, and ambled around the colossal circular base of the mound.

More strange school buildings came into view: a semi-circular hall of brick with huge classical columns on one side; a white 1930s block with weird elongated windows; a motley array of toilets and carpentry sheds, and an enormously long hut of corrugated iron with a warning on the door suggesting it was a rifle range. He passed a rose garden, too, with a chapel towering proud above it, lofty, with a dainty spire, and glimpsed a new building going up inside a paddock of fence and razor-wire. But the whole place was deserted. If it had been term-time, he supposed, it would have been buzzing with -

He stopped.

There was a straggling line of cheap concrete steps leading straight to the top of the mound. In the seventeenth century they had seen fit to cut a long, spiral path for leisured aristocrats to coil their way to the summit by a half-mile walk. More recently, it seemed, people had been in more of a hurry. The concrete steps cut clean across the old path and took the shortest possible route.

But Jo told himself he couldn't be bothered. It was hot, the climb was very steep, and what was so great about the top of a mound?

"I'm the King of the Castle," he muttered sarcastically, trying to convince himself that he wasn't fascinated.

And then he noticed something else.

A few yards further on, built into the very side of the mound, was a bizarre square structure made of flints, the entrance guarded by ornate iron gates. He walked on and peered through the bars. It was the most extraordinary thing, almost laughable: a grotto, the walls and ceiling completely covered by huge, pearly sea-shells embedded in mortar. It was like the setting for a hideous pink painting of sea-nymphs and mermaids.

"At home with Neptune," thought Jo. Grott-o was about right.

At his feet was a flagstone, with an inscription that read:

"*Made by Lady Hertford, c.1735.*"

The grotto, it seemed, was nothing more than an amazing expression of eighteenth-century bad taste. It was divided into three dinky little chambers: the central cave, directly in front of the doors, and a more private alcove on either side, dipping round beyond easy vision. Jo half wanted to go in, exercise in hideousness though the grotto was. But the gates were -

"Oh."

No. They *weren't* locked. As he pulled they swung open, creaking on rusting hinges. He looked down at his hand, marked with a streak of rust and grime. And then, with a certainty that he couldn't explain, like the instinctive knowledge that a decision is right, Jo suddenly knew that to go inside would have consequences, would be in some way dangerous. Everything told him to stay outside.

He stepped in.

An old fag-packet had been chucked under a marble bench: the grotto was evidently an upmarket alternative to the bikesheds. Spiders were fond of the place, too, their webs stretching from scallop to conch. It was soily, mossy, grimy but, he had to admit it, kind of splendid in its dotty, romantic way. As he turned into the

21

left-hand alcove he thought there'd be a -

"Oh God! Sorry!"

He hadn't seen her sitting there till then.

Jo had blurted out the apology, but a moment later was annoyed - annoyed that she hadn't seen fit to make her presence known.

He shuffled, awkward. She made no attempt to break the silence. The position of her head suggested she was staring straight at him, but she sat as if frozen. Not a movement, not the slightest tremor, did she make. Jo felt he ought to say something.

"I - I didn't see you there."

The silence that followed his second utterance seemed even stranger than the first. He couldn't see her properly in the shadowy alcove. Her feet were bare. Her skirt was hitched up above her knees - that much he couldn't help noticing. Her hair was long and straight. But her face, somewhere in that hood of hair, he couldn't see at all. Should he just walk out and leave her in her apparent trance? He couldn't explain why, but he felt that would be like a retreat. But to approach her in this secret place might seem threatening: she might scream and create a scene. Then inspiration came: he asked her a perfectly logical question.

"Are you okay?"

He wasn't expecting a reply. But it came. Her hands suddenly began to move in a wide-spreading gesture, then returned to her own belly. And out of the shadow that was her face came a voice that seemed familiar, saying:

"They don't know who I am. They don't see me at all. Yet I give them everything. Don't let them ravage me. You must make them see."

Her whole body suddenly rose from its seat.

"I need your help, boy. Save me from them!"

Jo gasped and recoiled. But the faceless woman stopped. Then she squatted, hands still on belly, and Jo realised, to his horror, that her belly was round, *very* round, and the image of his mother at his sister's birth flashed into his mind. He shouted wordlessly and ran from the place, flinging the iron gate shut behind him.

* * *

"Dad, when are we going to see Mum again?"

Jo delved into his packet of crisps to look casual. His father plonked his pint mug down and wiped a line of froth from his thin lip.

"When she comes down off her high horse and'll speak to me again."

"Have you rung her?"

His father picked up his mug before replying. Then he said:

"I've been much too busy, Jo. She's got naff-all to do as usual. If she wanted to see us she could come down here any time. She knows where we are."

"She's got Kate to look after."

"No problem - we'd just rent another room here in the hotel."

"No," said Jo, "I didn't mean that. I meant she hasn't got naff-all to do."

"Oh God, you sound like a New Man. What, looking after a baby's hard work, is it?"

"Yes."

"She should try archaeology. This is a dig and a half, Jo, I'll tell you. I reckon I've lost about half a stone already: I was sweating like a pig all afternoon. Great showers this place has got, though. I don't suppose *you*'ve had one yet?"

Jo ignored the question and said: "I think I'll send her a postcard."

His father took an angry mouthful, glanced around the hotel bar to check for privacy, then leaned forward and hissed:

"Look, what is it? Since when are you a Mummy's boy? The last few months before your mother and I broke up you hardly said a word to her. It really got to her, if you want to know. It was one

23

of the reasons she thought you should come with me."

Jo felt it like a body-blow. "Is that what she said?"

"She didn't want you sloping around the house, lost in your little world."

"That's not true!" said Jo, refusing to let the tears come. "It's just she had her hands full with Kate!"

"Jealousy, eh?" his father said with an incongruous laugh. "Elbowed aside by the new one? Dead right, Jo. She couldn't find time for anyone else."

Jo struck back. "That's what she used to say about *you*."

"What?"

"That you were never there - all you ever cared about was work."

"What did she think brought in the money? She was happy enough to have that."

"That's not the impression *I* got," said Jo. "She didn't give a monkey's about the new car, and she said what was the point of the poncy carpet and furniture with a one-year-old?"

"Do you want another Coke - dissolve a few more teeth?"

Another blow, but Jo kept going. He was going to ask the question. He took a deep breath and, trying to sound calm and grown up, he said: "Why did you and Mum split up? What went wrong?"

His father finished a three-gulp drink, put the mug down squarely on its mat and said: "She was a neurotic cow. Will that do?"

Jo was determined not to cry. "Don't you miss her? And Kate?"

At that, a strange glare, half pain, half rage, flashed across his father's face. He looked down at his almost empty glass, and very soft and very dark he said:

"Why should I care about *Kate*?"

For a moment Jo didn't understand. He stared, incredulous. Then a chasm of awful possibility opened before him. Did he

24

mean...? But before he could ask the obvious, terrible question, his father swirled the last mouthful at the bottom of his glass and said:

"You'll soon learn."

On a mantelpiece a clock chimed jollily.

"Learn what?"

"You'll understand one day. Men and women weren't meant to live together. In fact, I'm having second thoughts about sending you to that College - it's co-ed; you'd be better off sticking with your own kind."

"What do you mean, sending me to the College?" said Jo in sudden alarm. "What, you mean that school here? Marlborough?"

"Yeah, I thought I'd mentioned it when - "

"You've *never* mentioned it!"

"It'll cost a packet, of course," his father breezed on, gazing indifferently into his empty glass. "But it's about the best that money can buy - big public school, you know, right up there with Eton, Harrow, that lot - and obviously it's going to be better for you to be at a boarding school from now on - home life isn't going to be easy whichever way we swing it."

"Thanks for telling me." Jo shoved his Coke across the table. He felt as though he might be sick.

"God, here we go again," said his father, agitating coins in his corduroy pocket. "Not happy being on a brilliant dig. Now not happy being sent to a brilliant school."

"I don't like the place."

"How can you possibly know?"

Jo looked down at the table. It was glass-topped, and in the strange, low light of the hotel bar it sent a dark reflection of his own furrowed face. But all he could see was the grotto, and the round-bellied woman.

"No," he said, and for a moment he couldn't quite breathe. "I mean I don't like the *place*."

3. The Hill and the Ditch

The dig was making painfully slow progress - in Jo's eyes if no-one else's. A large pile of chalk rubble, devoid of anything approaching an artefact, had now taken shape, but it was certainly no spectator sport, this archaeology lark. Marlborough's wide historic High Street held no great appeal for Jo, either, filled as it was with what looked like tourists stopping off on the way to Bath - as the gentry had done *en route* to taking the waters three centuries before - to potter into flowery tea rooms and shops full of pointless "gifts".

But what he least fancied was hanging around the mound.

Money was no object, his father kept telling him, so he got some cash off his dad and went and hired a bike. In all directions but one the roads out of Marlborough seemed to set off up alarmingly steep hills, so Jo stuffed the ankles of his jeans inside his socks and pushed himself off along the road the Georgian gentry would have taken in their coaches - westward and level down the old Bath Road.

The road meandered, broad and easy. That was the problem. Cars and lorries tore past in a dusty thunder, treating it like a motorway, and after a couple of miles of near-death experiences Jo turned his handlebars to the right and started pedalling into the hills along a white chalk track - bumpy, rutted but less menacing.

He found himself entering an extraordinary landscape.

26

The silence was total, all traffic noise baffled by the high green ridges, their contours smooth as human limbs. Passing up a long, slow valley, he might have been riding between the legs of a recumbent giant, sunning herself in the August heat, legs that opened into a field of barley, deep and long-bearded, which even urban Jo could sense was ready for harvest now. He sensed, too, that he shouldn't stray into such private and unfamiliar territory.

He turned aside, struggling up a steep farm track and over into another valley, this one inhabited by an immense flock of stones - massive flat boulders, looking for all the world like sheep cropping the pasture of the valley floor. And:

"Rabbits," he said to himself and his bike, surprised to see so many so nerveless in the broad blue day.

There were real sheep among the stone flock, and Jo startled several by his movement before one startled him by its stillness: he braked hard before a carcass, wrecked and ragged, its eyes and guts gouged and savaged. He gulped, and looked around at the ridges, the clumps of trees, the thorn brakes, as if expecting an ambush; the sudden death amongst so much life felt ominous. But there was life amongst the death as well: ants teemed in the sheep's belly, flies flicked at bloody sockets. Jo grunted and shuddered, and pushed away.

He rode on again, following no direction, seeing no-one. He passed through a gate or two, pedalled down several easy tracks and then tested the mountain bike's spokes and frame by bumping wildly over open slopes, an obstacle course of tussock and mole-hill.

Then he crested a final sweeping rise of green and there below him, to his astonishment, was an even bigger version of his father's mound in Marlborough: an immense, perfectly round hill, truly as big as an Egyptian pyramid. It stood, inexplicably to Jo, in a patch of unremarkable, low-lying ground beside a busy A-road.

He was annoyed. After hours away from any thought of his dad and the dig, here was an arch-reminder. This must be the

Silbury Hill that his father had mentioned - another pile of prehistoric pointlessness. He'd said himself that archaeologists had already done their work here, and found nothing buried in or under its vast body, but now he was wasting his time on its sibling a few miles to the east.

But Jo had to admit it was impressive. Its size was all the plainer when he noticed a human figure standing on the top: it provided a measure. And it suddenly threw an image into his mind of an Aztec atop a mighty temple, offering a dripping heart to the Sun, or a warlord in a sword-and-sorcery tale, worshipping some savage sky-god.

And then the figure waved. Jo couldn't tell if it was waving to him, and he wouldn't have waved back anyway. But the idea of going to the top strangely appealed, and he free-wheeled down a bumpy slope and found his way to the foot of Silbury Hill.

It was all fenced off. Climbing was clearly not encouraged. And it was incredibly steep. But he could see a winding path of white snaking its way up the western side, the chalk exposed where many pairs of feet had evidently felt impelled to break the law. There was no question of taking his bike up there, and he had no padlock, so he checked that no-one was watching and hid it under a hawthorn bush. Then he crossed the surrounding fence at a point where people before him had trampled down the wire, and set off up the chalky track. It was all the more exciting for being illegal, he thought, and then, after a few brief spurts of thigh- and calf-straining effort, he found himself confronted by the colossal anti-climax of the summit: a circular patch of thick, rough, tufty, empty grass.

"Not even much of a view," he muttered. Lying as low as it did, the vast mound of Silbury was no higher than the surrounding hills.

He stomped across the grass until he reached the exact middle.

And then, suddenly, he realised how very tired he was. He'd been cycling for hours, for the first time in ages, and had drunk nothing and eaten nothing since breakfast. Now it must be late in the afternoon. The heat had gone out of the sun, and in fact, as he noticed with a touch of worry, a front of bruise-black cloud was advancing from the west.

"What an idiot," he said to himself. "Why did you keep going so far?"

But the thought of going straight back down was too much. Jo flopped with a great exhalation and slumped back into the deep, dusty green. He closed his eyes for a moment or two, stretched arms and legs to finger- and toe-tips, then relaxed every muscle and let his weight sink into the earth. Great. Absolutely brilliant. He lay, basking, and smiled as the grass tickled his neck, soothing it where it had caught the sun. Calm. Easy.

"So you came."

This sudden voice jolted him upright. A figure was standing alarmingly close, its face lost against the sky-glare. It was wearing a hat with two erect feathers, and a long coat, lank and shabby.

"I thought you would come."

It was a man. It moved around Jo, and stopped beside his waist. Jo hurriedly shuffled to his knees.

"No need to get up."

"What?" said Jo.

"You need a rest, don't you?"

"Do I?"

"Oh yes."

Jo was no longer dazzled by the sky, and he could see the man's face clearly. It was hungry and battered. Wisps of greasy hair stuck out from under the hat. Several days' growth of beard and moustache shadowed the jaws and upper lip. And the man said: "I waved to you but you didn't wave back."

There was nothing in the Welsh-tinged voice to suggest that this was a joke. Jo sensed the man was actually offended. It was ridiculous.

"Sorry," he said. "I'm really sorry - I - I didn't know it was you."

"How could you?" said the man. "You'd never seen me before."

Jo hesitated. What was the right answer?

"No," he said, neutrally. "No, quite."

And he was just about to get to his feet when the man abruptly dropped down beside him, squatting on his haunches.

"So," the man said, looking straight at him. "Troubled, then." It was a statement, not a question.

"What d'you mean?"

"You're running away."

"I'm - ?"

"Running away," said the man.

"What makes you say that?"

"Well, look at you. So anxious and heavy-browed. And nothing about you of the cyclist. Where's your hi-tech water-bottle, or your packet of sustaining snacks? You've come all this way and not a crumb or drop by way of refreshment."

The man's lilting intonation was as strange as his speech.

"I've not come far at all, actually," said Jo, trying to sound casual, "and I'm just about to - "

"Yes you have," the man cut in. "Miles. I can tell by the sweat." To Jo's alarm the man's nostrils were flaring, scenting him like an animal. "But you'll soon be showered, don't worry."

"What?" said Jo. This was getting freaky.

"Well look," the man said, and he nodded towards the west. The great bruise in the sky was spreading rapidly nearer. "I love to see the rain come."

And indeed, beneath the bruise a vast, delicate gauze of rain was drifting towards them.

"If enough falls you'll see her properly."

"See who?" said Jo.

The man looked back at him, then sprang to his feet.

"I'll show you!" he said. "Follow me. Come on! Come on!"

Suddenly the man was as a boy, bounding across the grass towards the western edge of Silbury's round top. He turned back and beckoned excitedly. Jo felt he ought to humour him, so he heaved himself up and trudged over with an air of determined indifference to stand beside the stranger.

"There! Look!"

He was pointing earnestly down to the bottom of the hill. Jo looked.

"Sorry," he said. "I - I can't see anyone."

"The ditch," said the man. "You can see her wondrous body in the outline of the ditch. There's a lot of water left there from the heavy rains this year, and if we have another downpour she'll appear in all her glory."

Jo didn't know how to handle this at all. Then the man turned and looked at him again, straight in the eyes.

"You can't see her, can you? Worry not, you're not alone."

Jo decided to be honest. "Look, I haven't the faintest idea who you're talking about."

"The Lady," the man said in a reverent whisper. "The Lady of the Lake."

The rain was suddenly upon them. Not heavy, but saturating, an intense, deep, refreshing wetness. In seconds Jo's hair was flat upon his head and dripping over his brows and nose. His shirt clung to his back and shoulders. The man was singing. Jo had no idea what: it didn't sound remotely like English. The voice veered wildly from high to low, and was accompanied by flailing gestures and washing of the face with soaking hands.

"Look, I - I think I'm going to go back down," Jo called across to him. "I'll see you." The man didn't so much as turn to look. "Complete nutter," Jo muttered to himself. "I think I'll take my chance!" And he scurried quietly across the grass to the chalky path. Just as he was about to climb back down he glanced behind to make sure and: "Oh no!" The nutter was watching him. Jo started to run –

"Ah!"

- and then wished he hadn't. The rain had made the chalk lethally smooth. Before he'd gone three steps his feet shot from under him, and –

"Oh God!" he cried, as he pitched from the path –

"No!"

- and rolled, pounding, rib over rib, down the sheering side of the massive mound. He had no sense of hitting the ditch.

* * *

He was underwater. A storming in his ears as he swam, floundered, panicked, beating his feet in a frenzy, unsure which was up or down. His shirt billowed around his face. Then, in his total blindness, something stroked his legs and gripped his ankle. He roared with his mouth tight shut, beat his shirt down, opened his eyes. It was weed - long, waving fronds of shining green; and in his wrestling panic he was binding himself more tightly by the second. He roared through his nose, emptying his lungs. He kicked and heaved, wrenched with all his might; he was desperate to breathe now, his ribs had to move, his lungs had to fill; but he knew that a breath would be a body full of water and an instant death. He kicked and tore and flailed again. It was the final time, because as he twisted round to wrench the harder, he found himself staring into the face of a woman. Her hair wafting gently in the water, she was looking at him without alarm, without a smile. She just stared, and he calmed. She reached out, took his hands, and effortlessly drew him from the weed. She was carrying him upward, and in a moment he broke the surface and she held him head and shoulders above the water. He breathed, gasped and swallowed air. But as he looked down to see her again, other arms were seizing him, hauling and man-handling him, and with a bruising thump he was hitting wood.

"You all right, boy?"

There were two men in the boat, and one had instantly gone back to the oars. The other looked down at Jo with brief concern, but in seconds was more interested in what was over the side.

"Back this way," he was saying to his mate. "Just here. That's it."

The other stopped rowing and peered down.

"Is it her?"

"Yep."

There was a long pause while they stared fixedly at the water. The immense belly of the hill rose above them. The water was completely still.

"She's gone, ha'n't she?"

The other nodded.

They looked back at Jo with the deepest sorrow.

"Damn it," the first one said. "I reckon she's gone."

Jo just stared. "I didn't know her," he said. "It wasn't my Mum."

They looked at him in puzzlement, and waited for him to say more. He looked back blankly.

"I don't know who she was," he said; and then:

"Over here!"

The call wasn't from the oarsman; it was a distance away; and as Jo strained to look round he saw a figure standing on the bank of the ditch, waving.

"The nutter," Jo muttered to himself.

"Bring him over here," came the Welsh-tinged cry. "He's with me."

Jo slumped in the boat-bottom, too exhausted to resist.

4. The Motorbike

When he woke he couldn't move his arms. For a panic-stricken moment he was wrestling again; but this time he freed himself in seconds: only a blanket pinioned him - someone had wrapped him up to sleep. And a fire of twigs and branches was crackling on the grass beside him. It was night, and wild shadows were dancing all over the side of an old caravan.

"All right?"

It was the nutter.

"Yeah," said Jo blearily. "Yes, I think so."

"Here - have a cup of tea."

Jo sat up shakily, and took fumbling hold of an old enamel mug; he flinched at the sudden heat, but steered his nose into the rising steam and drank.

"That was a fall to wonder at!" the man said, taking off his feathered hat and scratching his scalp. "I'm amazed you're in one piece!"

"If the water hadn't been so deep...," Jo replied.

There was a pause. Quite nearby an owl hooted.

"Deep?" said the man. "It wasn't deep. Only just enough to swim a swan."

Jo looked at him.

"The rain wasn't enough to fill the ditch," the man continued

34

in his sing-song rhythm. "When it does, it makes the blessed shape of the Lady. I wanted you to see her. Our great Mother, the hill her belly, full and wonderful, her - "

"I went right in," Jo said, ignoring the crazed ramblings, "and got my legs caught in the weeds. Then a woman pulled me out and those men got me into their boat and - "

"Boat? What boat?"

"Oh for God's sake," said Jo, "there were two blokes who rowed me over to you. They - "

"They were in a tractor."

Jo couldn't cope with this. "No, I mean the - "

"They were in a tractor. I saw them. They drove into the ditch and picked you up. But I reckon they were more interested in their sheep."

"What? Look - "

"A ewe had wandered into the ditch and got stuck. Drowned, she did. They just left her there. Typical. Drink your tea."

Jo took a mouthful and stared at the fire, trying to work it out. If it hadn't been deep water, and it hadn't been a boat, and the men had been talking about a sheep, had the woman been -

"*Who* was it you said pulled you out?"

Was madness catching? Had his contact with this nutter on the top of the hill been enough to send him over the edge in more ways than one? He wanted no more to do with this man with his grubby beard and lank coat, and he certainly didn't want to be hanging round a rusting caravan in the middle of nowhere. He put the mug down and started to get up. To his alarm the man grabbed his arm.

"Don't do that," said Jo. "Let go of me."

"No need to be alarmed. I think you're special."

Special? This was too much. It was scary now.

"I said let go."

"I told you you'd see her," the man said, "but I didn't mean you to get *that* close!"

"Look, I really don't know what you're talking about, and I'll be honest - you're scaring me."

"Oh it's nothing to be scared about. It's special, seeing as you've seen. What did she look like?"

Jo stopped struggling. He could see the woman's face in his mind's eye. And it would be good to have an explanation.

"Had you seen her before?" the man asked.

Had he? Now he came to think of it, he wasn't sure. And as her face came back to mind, over her shoulder peered another face - except it wasn't a face but a shadow, with long straight hair and arms spreading wide, about to speak to him in that weird grotto.

"Yes," Jo said, distantly. "Yes, I think I had - or, or someone quite like her."

"Brilliant!" the man said, and he clapped his hands like an excited child. "Stupendous!"

"Please," said Jo. "What's happening?"

"You can see!" the man said, a beaming smile in the firelight; and then, with something approaching reverence, he murmured: "Not many can see the past and see the gods."

Jo stared at him; then said: "I'm very tired. You'll have to take this gently."

The man sat down. And with back straight, head high, he took a deep breath and said:

"The gods are everywhere. It's just that they've been forgotten. Some have been so forgotten that they've died. Or are dying at this very moment. Dying of neglect. Their being, you see, depends on our devotion to them. But maybe they could be reawakened if we had the will."

Jo sat in silence, acutely aware that a week ago he'd have laughed at this. Now he felt on the edge of a whole new world.

A twig squeaked and snapped in the fire; a moth flopped raggedly through the glow.

Then suddenly the man's head turned. His smile vanished and he sat dead still.

"What's the matter?" said Jo.

"Sssh!"

Everything was motionless. Not a breath of wind, not a rustle in the trees. Just snaps and cracks in the wood-fire. Gently, with the most surprising feline stealth, the man rose from the ground and crept towards his caravan. To Jo's amazement and dismay he then stooped and picked up a crowbar, and stood with his back pressed to the corner of the 'van, poised like the slickest L.A. cop, ready to strike. Jo didn't know what to do: shall I sit here like a lemon and watch, he thought, or take my chance and run? He shifted the blanket, ready to rise, and instantly the man's finger flashed to his lips, ordering silence. On the other side of the 'van, something scuffed the ground. A yard further along, it made contact with a bottle and there was a hissing curse at the jangling ring. Then there was a second voice, whispering a word inaudibly. Another step and rustle, and another. They were moving along the far side of the 'van, and away from the corner where the man stood poised. In samurai silence he glided round the side and disappeared from Jo's sight. A pause. Then an explosion of noise, a scream, a crash as someone hit the back of the 'van, and then... laughter.

"You idiot!" came a voice. "You scared the whatsit out o' me!"

"Good grief!" said another. "Where did *you* come from?"

And two tall, slim figures came stumbling from behind the caravan, through the long grass and into the firelight. The man was following them, a high-pitched laugh ringing out, performing an array of slashes with the crowbar like a black belt martial artist.

The two new figures stood still, looking at Jo.

"Who's this?" one of them said.

Jo's first thought was they must be freezing - just t-shirts and jeans they wore - and they might have been commandos, dressed all in black and with dirt smeared on their cheeks and foreheads as if for camouflage. But what struck Jo next was the strange nobility of their faces: they wouldn't have looked out of place in shining armour.

"I don't know who he is come to think of it," the nutter said, "we've not been introduced!" And he laughed again; and tossing his crowbar aside he walked straight over to Jo as if nothing had happened, his arm outstretched to offer a handshake, and: "Hello! I'm Dag."

"Jo," said Jo, not thinking to lie, and shook his hand.

"And this is Gareth and Mort."

"Short for Morton," said one, "but I can't call myself that. Poncy or what? Oh, *Morton!*" he said, putting on a posh voice, *"what a simply spiffing name!* Jo's good. I like that. Short for Joseph, though - that's dodgy."

"No," said Jo, though he didn't see the problem. "Joel."

"Oh, wow! Not too many of those about! If I had a name as good as that I wouldn't change it. *Joel.*"

"What about Dag?" said Jo. "What's that short for?"

The man with the grubby beard looked up and said: "Dagonet."

Jo expected the other two to laugh: *he* certainly wanted to. But there wasn't a flicker: they were unconcerned, their attention already elsewhere - on the pan that Dag had just taken off the fire.

"Any to spare?" said Mort.

"Have I ever let you down?" Dag answered, and he started to spoon stuff on to a chipped enamel plate: huge lumps of vegetable in a kind of risotto. "But first you'll tell me what you were doing shuffling and scuffling behind my 'van."

"Didn't want to wake you - we thought you'd be asleep."

Jo suddenly realised that he hadn't given a thought to the time. He looked at his watch.

"Midnight," he said out loud.

"Certainly is," said Mort. "What are you doing out here at this time? Solo crop circles?"

"What?" said Jo. "Oh, no, no." Now that he came to think of it, it was a very good question. "I was out on a bike ride."

"He's had a bit of an adventure," Dag said.

"You're looking the worse for wear, I have to say," burbled Gareth with his mouth full. "Won't your folks be worried?"

Jo hadn't given a thought to *that*, either.

"Where are you from?" said Mort.

Jo went blank with the sudden worry.

"You okay?"

"My dad'll go mental," Jo replied. "Have you got a 'phone?"

"What, a mobile?" said Mort. There was a pause, and then all three roared with laughter, Mort spraying food from his mouth. Jo couldn't see the joke. "'Fraid not," Mort said at last, and putting on another posh voice he added: "No can do, chummy."

Gareth was looking sympathetic, though, and said: "Where's your dad, then?"

"In Marlborough. At the Merlin Hotel."

"Oh, *frightfully* nice," Mort chipped in.

"Staying there with your mum?" Gareth asked.

"No," said Jo, and with his voice and eyes giving it all away he added: "Not with Mum."

"Aha!" said Mort, seeing it at once. "The curse of the broken marriage strikes again, methinks!"

And Jo, realising he was going to have to stand up to the banter, said, trying to sound tough:

"Something like that, yeah."

"On holiday?" Gareth at least asked straight questions.

"Not exactly. Well, *I* am, I suppose. But my dad's working."

"Phenomenal beans, Dag," said Mort, wolfing down the veg. "Where d'you get 'em?"

Dag ignored the question and asked Jo: "What does he do, your dad?"

"He's an archaeologist. He's working on a dig."

For a moment everything stopped. Gareth and Mort looked at each other, forks poised halfway to mouths. Then they carried on.

"Interesting job," said Mort. "Digging up the jolly old past."

"Yes," said Jo, flatly.

They carried on eating, faces down. An owl hooted again. A few moments passed, with forks clattering on plates and Mort sniffing. Then Dag looked up at the moon, sickle-sharp, and said: "Is this the dig at Marlborough? At the mound?"

"Yes," Jo replied. "You know about it?"

"Yeah," said Mort, and sniffed again. They carried on eating for a moment, still not looking at Jo; then he added: "Yeah - saw it in the mighty Gazette. The Gazette and Herald - all the news you need. Unbeatable. All human life is there."

This time it was an ad man's voice he aped. If only he'd stop mucking around, thought Jo, maybe you could tell what he was thinking.

"So," said Mort, holding out his plate for a second helping, "we gonna take you back or what?"

"Can you?"

"We have the technology."

"Can you manage my bike as well?" Jo asked.

"Tricky, that. What we have, my dear chap, is a motorsickle." Mort switched from posh to American hillbilly in mid-sentence.

"Don't worry," said Gareth. "If Mort and I take you back for tonight, you can come back tomorrow and fetch it. Listen - lie down and rest while we finish this, then we'll sort it out."

"Right," said Jo. "Great. Thanks. But can we go quickly? He'll be going spare."

"In two shakes of a dog's whatsit," said Mort.

Jo lay back down with a huge sigh, and gazed up at the sky. The moon was hidden now, but in irregular breaks between high clouds he could see stars prickling. No sound, except the clatter and scrape of forks on enamel. His eyes blurred with tiredness.

A minute had passed when the clattering stopped and voices whispered. The three men were talking very fast. Jo couldn't make out a word of it, but the tone was clear: they were serious, earnest, even worried. Suddenly:

"No!" It was Dag, and he was angry. His voice returned to an agitated whisper before he burst out with: "Don't you dare! I tell you he's special."

That stupid word again. What *was* all this?

"Who's to say he's on their side?" Dag was muttering. "I tell you, he might be the one to stop them!"

There was silence now, very tense, until Mort sniffed - and then gave a snorting laugh and said: "Leave it to us. We know what to do." And getting up, he looked at Jo and: "Come on, then. Let's get on with it."

Everything told Jo not to go with them, to think of an excuse, to claim his dad wouldn't be that bothered, that he was often out this late - Jo? at fourteen? - that it could wait till tomorrow and he'd enjoy cycling back.

Dag was trying to smile jovially. "Off you go, then, Jo - they're ready for you now!"

Jo got up shakily, letting the blankets drop. For the first time he realised he wasn't in his own clothes - Dag had given him a weird purple shirt with a tie-dye pattern, and stained old denims that hung baggily round his bum. Dag saw him look and said: "Your own was soaking."

And he gestured to where Jo's stuff was hung along a rope between the caravan and a tree.

"Come back for it tomorrow? Same time as your bike?"

"No," said Jo. "I'll take them now."

Dag hesitated - it seemed he wanted to argue - but then decided to say: "Right. Yes. Probably for the best." And he turned to take them down.

Jo said: "Where is it? Their motorbike?"

"Oh," said Dag, and stopped, as Mort and Gareth looked at him. "Where's your bike, boys? Left it by the road?"

"Yeah," said Mort. "Yeah, that's it."

"Yes," said Dag. "By the road. Wouldn't want to bring it here, down by the spring."

"Chews up the ground," said Gareth. "Come on."

Jo was breathing very fast. He took his clothes from Dag and stood stock still, rooted.

"Come on," Gareth said again.

Jo peered at Dag for some kind of clue; Dag just smiled and gave a playful wave. Nutter. Then Mort took hold of his arm and said, emphatically: "*Come on!*"

Jo looked up at him, his mouth open, his heart thumping, and Mort said, like a jokey uncle: "Or we won't be there till breakfast!"

And Jo was being marched through the trees, away from the fire, away from the 'van. His feet were wet from his soaking shoes, a nettle burned across his hand, a bramble whipped across his face.

"Ow!"

"Little buggers, aren't they?"

Half pushed, half dragged, Jo stumbled his way through the darkness, in terror of what the next minutes would bring, until suddenly they came out of the trees and the moon gleamed down from behind a cloud. There, close to the road, right beside a hawthorn bush, right beside his own bike, was an old red motorcycle, and a sidecar that looked as if it had seen both world wars.

"Hop in," said Gareth. "I'll ride behind Mort."

"I could - I could just use my own bike," stammered Jo.

"No way, José," said Mort in his best Mexican. "No lights, amigo - and tyres caput."

He had a point. Someone had let Jo's tyres down. Given that he hadn't had a padlock, it was a miracle the bike was still there at all, and with two wheels and a saddle. Jo - relieved that at least the motorbike hadn't been a lie - nodded and climbed into the sidecar. Mort straddled the old red machine, Gareth leapfrogged up behind; a turn of the key, an almighty kick and they were off. And then, once they'd picked up speed:

"*I don't want a pickle -*

Just wanna ride on my motorsickle" -

Mort launched into an eccentric, warbling jingle.

*"And I don't want a tickle -
'Cos I'd rather ride on my motorsickle"* -

This was bizarre. Blasting through the Wiltshire wind at midnight, bellowing out a barmy country and western song. And Gareth joined in:

*"And I - don't wanna die!
Just wanna ride on my motorcy - "*

They paused in unison; then, exactly together:

" - cle!"

For the first time in ages, Jo laughed. Suddenly it was all too mad to be dangerous. He'd got them wrong.

The singing wasn't going to bother anyone - open country on both sides. And there was nothing on the road at all. A couple of minutes later Jo began to recognise it: he was retracing the way he'd cycled all those hours ago. He spotted the chalky track he'd turned down to get away from all the lorries. Yes. A few minutes more and they'd be back in Marlborough. But he didn't want it to stop now. This was fun! With the wind blowing wild through his tousled hair and tingling the down on his sunburnt skin he felt as elated, as reckless, as Toad on the open road. He laughed again, and grinned a wide, white smile at Gareth. Gareth smiled back.

Just then headlights flared in the distance as a car came over the brow of a hill. It drew nearer, and as it did, Jo heard Mort mutter, in sudden worry: "It just *had* to be."

It passed them in a fleeting glare, and Jo clearly saw the livery and the crest on the door. Police. Gareth was looking back.

"Are they?" said Mort.

"Yep."

The police car was stopping, and turning round.

"Right," said Mort, and opened the throttle. There was an almighty lurch and a guttural roar. The bike wasn't made to go at that speed, and the coupling to the sidecar creaked and strained. What was the problem? Was it because they weren't wearing helmets? Jo struggled to twist round and look behind. The headlights were following for sure.

"Hold tight." Just as they veered round a bend - so passing out of the police's sight - to Jo's amazement Mort switched off their own lights and swerved violently into a narrow lane. The sidecar had its wheel off the tarmac and blundered along the verge; Gareth swore as he pitched sideways and had to cling to Mort's back; and Mort fought like fury to keep the bike on the road. He did it. They surged and plunged over a hump-backed bridge - every wheel off the ground for a second before crunching back to earth - and then charged on blindly, no headlamp to light their way through the blackness.

"Turn the light back on!" he heard Gareth calling; but Mort said:

"Gotta make sure we've lost 'em!"

The moon beamed again through a gap in the clouds, and Mort braked hard: a crossroads, and an old wooden signpost with four pointing hands.

"Which way?"

"Marlborough'll be left," said Gareth. "Are they still behind us?"

Mort turned off the engine. Sudden, stunning silence. They sat very still, and listened. The faintest of breezes stirring the trees; the rustle of a tiny night-hunter in the grass. In the far distance, a car humming along the main road.

"Did it!" said Mort. "Lost 'em!" And he crowed quietly. "So...

Marlborough Ho!"

And he switched on the engine - and the lights - again, and turned left down another lane. Fences and hedges and trees passed by, and soon they were in a lightless village, pottering past houses, a school, a pub. They came to a sharp bend where another lane joined, and Mort said: "See where we are?"

Gareth nodded.

"What d'you reckon? Back on the main road? Or down here?"

"Keep to the back way," said Gareth; and off to the right they went, into even deeper darkness as trees canopied the narrow lane.

They know the way well, thought Jo. What on earth would ever bring them up here?

It was even more puzzling when the lane suddenly ended; two footpaths forked away right and left, one to a little flinty church, the other towards high-fenced tennis courts. It was towards the courts that Mort turned, and very slowly, in a growling first gear, he puttered the machine along the stony track - and turned off the lights again. A few moments later another light appeared - a bright glare away to the left. Mort stopped and looked across.

"Hmm," said Mort. "I do believe a cage has been rattled."

Jo, wondering what this could mean, followed Mort's gaze and began to recognise the outline of trees and buildings in the near-distance, and realised that the glare came from bright lamps blazing on the side of the Marlborough mound - at just about the very spot, unless he was much mistaken, where his dad was digging.

"Know where you are now?" Mort said to Jo. "We'll leave you here, I think. See you."

He meant it. A quick jerk of the head made it clear that Jo's ride was over. He clambered out, and almost as soon as his feet touched the ground the bike and sidecar were heaving round and Mort and Gareth - their faces still blackened, Jo suddenly registered - were rattling away up the track.

As it happened, Jo didn't know how to get to the mound from there, and he could hear water running loudly over a weir nearby. He wondered if a river would cut him off, but he followed his nose and came upon a footbridge, water tumbling fast beneath. He began to run - he didn't know why - and raced over the bridge, along a path beside a lake and into the grass and trees and maze of buildings below the looming mound. Round towards the light he ran, until a minute later he found himself back in civilisation. In the glare of three huge arc-lamps people were scurrying and calling, waving and pointing – an agitated hive at fully half-past midnight. A little way above him, on the side of the Stone Age mound, his dad's team of archaeologists seemed very excited. But as he stood a few yards away, getting his breath back from his run, Jo realised there weren't a lot of smiles around. And the first voice he heard was his dad's, and he was barking in exasperation.

"What the hell did they do this for?" he was saying. "Two days' work all gone for nothing!"

If his dad was in this mood, what would he be like when Jo appeared? Should he just slip away back to the hotel, and somehow brazen it out in the morning?

"I mean, what *is* this?" he could hear his dad say. "Some kind of practical joke?"

"Well, there's not a lot we can do now," someone else said, trying to calm him. "Might as well sleep on it and have a proper look at it tomorrow."

"What's the forecast?"

"Fine. Warm and sunny."

A sigh of resignation from his dad; then, sullen: "Yeah, okay, come on."

The team started to shuffle down the steep bank, and suddenly the arc-lamps went out. Jo's eyes couldn't adjust before:

"Jo! Is that you?"

Now he was going to be for it.

"Erm - yes, Dad - I'm sorry I've - "

"Where have you been? I was starting to get... No, Don!" his father said, distracted by an assistant to his left. "Leave it there for now." Then he turned back to Jo. "You can tell me your story later. Good God: what the hell are you wearing?"

And that was the extent of his dad's concern.

5. The Tunnel

A tense, early breakfast, Jo's dad knocking back coffee and looking repeatedly at his watch, while Jo wolfed down bacon, eggs, sausages, mushrooms, tomatoes and fried bread and then set about the toast.

"I take it they didn't feed you, then?" his dad suddenly said.

"Mmm?"

"The people you say looked after you."

His dad stroked his chin and looked strangely at him. Jo couldn't understand why he didn't believe his story about an accident on the hired bike, blacking out and finding himself soaked by the rain and being gifted the t-shirt and baggy denims by a couple of kindly hikers. It all sounded plausible enough, he thought.

"They had great taste, I must say," his dad said with a smirk. "Tie-dye went out of fashion when I was your age."

Nor could Jo understand why he didn't want to tell his dad the truth about anything or anyone he'd encountered -

"Come on, Jo, hurry up - I've got to get down there."

- or why his dad was in fact so unconcerned that he'd been lost till well past midnight.

"Did you tell Mum?" Jo asked, peeling the fiddly foil from a portion of butter.

"What?"

"That I was lost."

"Your mother?" His dad snorted. "You must be joking! Can you imagine the panic? She'd've been down here screaming that it was my fault. Jo, you can't possibly need toast as well."

Jo defiantly finished spreading the marmalade and took a huge mouthful, and through it, while his dad huffed and looked at his watch again, he said: "You still haven't told me the problem."

"Up at the dig?"

"Mmm."

A waitress arrived to clear most of their plates, delicately collecting the cutlery so that the Edwardian silence of the breakfast room was not disturbed, and Jo's dad waited for her to go before leaning forward and whispering, as if the deepest secret: "It's unbelievable."

And he shook his head.

"What is?"

"Someone's filled in the hole."

"What do you mean?"

"I mean someone's filled in the hole," his dad said, his voice rising in exasperation. "Not a complex concept, is it? Some idiot came back after dark when we'd all gone home and blocked up the tunnel we've been digging."

"Good job you hadn't done much, then," said Jo. He hadn't meant any offence, but his dad's eyes widened in fury.

"Wrong. Wrong again. Just because you want everything done at a hundred miles an hour - " He stopped, not wanting to go down the old road about Jo's generation and instant gratification, and began again quietly: "It was going amazingly fast, you'll be surprised to know."

"Find anything?" said Jo, enjoying the marmalade.

"Shut up and listen. We'd only gone in a few yards when we hit another tunnel."

Jo stopped eating. He could tell this was important.

"Someone's done it before, you see," his dad said, and put his hand to his mouth as if he felt sick. "I'd no idea - there's no record of any excavation. It must be ages old. It slopes down diagonally, straight towards the centre of the base."

"And you've been down?"

"Good God, of course not."   He seemed to be almost sweating. "The tunnel's ancient - it could collapse at any second if someone started blundering down."

"So what were you going to do?" said Jo, gently laying down some half-eaten toast.

"Send in a camera to see what's down there - and if it's worth having, get it out."

From the kitchen came a crash and nervous laughter as china shattered on the floor.

"How would you do that - get it out, I mean?"

"We'll find a way," his father said; and then quietly added: "Whatever it takes."

"Well, yes," said Jo, and he gulped and cleared his throat, "but you wouldn't want to - well..." He stopped, not knowing how to finish the sentence.

"What?" said his father.

And suddenly the words of the woman in the grotto echoed in Jo's head, and he said: "You wouldn't want to - *ravage* it, would you?"

His dad gave one of his lop-sided smiles, amused at the strange choice of word. He drummed his fingers on the table, then looked at his watch again. He didn't reply.

"Well," Jo continued, clearing his throat again, "it's no big deal, is it? Someone blocking it up. Just clear it away and carry on."

"The point is they're saboteurs. They could come back and foul things up again any time."

"How do you know?" said Jo. "It could just be - "

"They left a message."

"Oh."

Jo waited. His dad picked up a napkin and needlessly dabbed his mouth.

"What," Jo prompted, "you mean on paper?"

"A load of New Age nonsense. For them, anything neolithic's a great sacred cow. They wander round hugging stones and dancing in crop circles and think they know the secret of life."

"What did they say?"

His dad tossed the napkin gently on to the table and said:

"Let sleeping gods lie."

A pause, then he snorted, as if cueing Jo to laugh, but Jo was staring down at the mess on his plate.

"Good, isn't it?" his dad said in scorn; then breezily: "There are two explanations: either they're so sad they really think Merlin's down there, or..."

He paused hammily, waiting for Jo to ask; and when he didn't, he added: "Or they're dyslexic."

He chuckled to himself, enjoying his own punchline.

* * *

As they rounded the corner of the College's science block, Jo's dad stopped dead.

"What the hell do this lot want?"

A substantial crowd had gathered at the foot of the mound, and Jo and his dad had to weave their way through a pushchair or two, several rucksacks and a number of amateur photographers.

"What's going on, Annie?" he asked one of his team, a university student who, far from troubled, seemed to be enjoying the celebrity.

"The local Tourist Information have got wind of it," she said, "and they're sending people to look!"

Jo's dad flung his head back in disbelief. "Oh, for - "

"It seems quite a few go into the Information Office asking about 'Merlin's Mound'," Annie explained. "They can't believe their luck that there's something actually happening here!"

Another of the team, bearded and permanently-jumpered Dave, came up. "They probably think it's set up for visitors," he said, "like a Civil War re-enactment!"

Jo's dad gave a snort, but it was totally unamused.

"This whole area's a theme park," Dave continued, in a voice Jo thought surprisingly squeaky for such a big-chested man. "One of the Tourist Information blokes told me they have Japanese tourists going in to ask about crop circles...in March! 'Sorry, chum, not at the moment.' '*Why* no clop circles?' 'Because no clops!'"

Annie wobbled as she roared with laughter, but Jo's dad wasn't even listening. "Any word from the police?" he asked.

"Yes," said Dave. "The College security guy - nice bloke - said he saw two men on the mound about half past ten. When he flashed his torch at 'em they were off like a shot, and a minute or two later he's fairly sure it's them leaving on a motorbike and sidecar - "

Jo started, but was completely unsurprised.

" - a vintage job, apparently, straight out of the ark. The police were up and down the A4 for an hour or so, and saw it coming *back* towards Marlborough - a bit strange - and when they went after 'em they acted '*hin a very suspicious mannah*' and gave 'em the slip. A real car chase - exciting stuff!"

"Did *you* see any of this, Jo?" his dad asked suddenly.

"Mmm?" said Jo, trying to sound casual.

"On your way back? You were out late enough. Did you see an old motorbike and sidecar?"

Jo turned and, looking his father straight in the eye, said:
"No."

* * *

For the tourists, the novelty of watching archaeologists shovelling had worn off - and the day had worn on. The team beavered away in privacy, reopening the tunnel and making preparations for sending a camera into the depths of the mound. In the late afternoon an express delivery van came rolling up with the equipment, its exhaust hanging dense and stinking in the heat-haze. Jo's dad opened the cases and whooped.

"Look at this!" he called, and the team gathered round. "State-of-the-art or what!"

"Merlin, mate," said a lanky student called Richie, "here we come!"

But an hour later, with everyone poised and ready to go, consternation.

"Oh I don't believe this," Dave wheezed in his squeaky voice. "They've only gone and sent the wrong lens."

"You're joking," said Annie.

"If only. We won't be able to see a frigging thing."

Jo's father swore and flung down his hat. "Damnation! This is..." He swore again. "So what do we do?"

Dave gave an asthmatic sigh and said: "I'll have to drive over to Oxford and sort it out myself. God they're hopeless."

Five minutes later, as Dave's car churned away over gravel and off towards the road, Jo's dad mopped some sweat from his neck and said:

"Another damned night, that's the trouble. The morons'll probably be back. We'll have to mount guard."

Shifts were allotted, the team dividing into pairs for hour-long stints. But they were an odd number, so Jo said: "I'll join in if you want, Dad."

His dad raised his eyebrows in theatrical surprise, and was on the point of making an acid remark by reflex when he thought better of it.

"Okay," he said. "Okay. That would be very helpful, Jo. Thank you."

For the first time in ages his father sounded warm. Jo glowed.

Then he instantly felt guilty: if his dad had known his motives for offering help... But no. He didn't care: he just wanted to be around to see what was going to happen. He was sure that Gareth and Mort would be back, but couldn't work out whether, having been spotted the night before at half-past ten, they'd be more likely to come at the same time - out of sheer defiance - or earlier, or later: they weren't exactly easy to second-guess. But he wasn't in a position to manipulate the time of his shift; his dad humiliated him in front of the team by saying:

"We'll put Jo on first or it'll be past his bedtime. Who wants the cushy one?"

Laughter on all sides. Jo ended up with Annie. Starting at eight. He felt small - and fed up, sure that nothing would happen that early.

But it got dark that night with surprising speed as dense cloud came scudding over, and Annie turned on the arc-lamps - partly to show marauders that the place was manned, and also simply for the sake of light. But it wasn't cold - in fact it was stickily humid - and he and Annie sat together in t-shirts and shorts on the side of the mound beside the tunnel, surrounded by drooping weeds and stillness.

Jo was surprised by the way she opened conversation.

"Tough on you, isn't he?"

"Mmm?"

"Your dad."

Jo looked away, not knowing what to say; but Annie continued: "Mind you, he's tough on everyone really: he's so uptight about this dig. I think he reckons it'll make his fortune - though I'd've thought he was well enough off already! Still, they always say: the more you have, the more you want." Jo shuffled and scratched at the earth, wanting her to stop, but she carried on: "You're not much like him, I have to say. Do you take after your mum?"

"It's hard to say," Jo answered quickly, and threw a stone

from hand to hand. And then he turned to her and said, quite strongly: "You know, you may be right, but he's still my Dad."

"Oh," said Annie, embarrassed. "Sorry."

Jo felt guilty again, and mumbled: "It's okay."

* * *

At that moment his dad had just walked into their hotel room, an unopened letter in his hand, and shut the door behind him. He looked briefly at the handwriting and the postmark, and was about to tear it open when he noticed another envelope, square and white, sitting in the middle of his bed, propped against what was obviously a bottle swathed in shiny silver wrapping paper. He stared for a moment, frowning as if troubled. Then he turned his back on it, opened his wardrobe door and thrust the first letter into the pocket of a suit-jacket hanging inside. He slammed the wardrobe shut, then stood, and sniffed; then strode past the bottle and the envelope and over to the window. He looked out into the failing light.

The High Street below was quiet and empty, until a man in a cycle helmet pedalled slowly past, chatting over his shoulder to a tiny helmeted child on a seat behind his saddle, who started shaking with laughter at his joke. Jo's dad watched them wobble and almost fall; the child found this hysterical. And on they went, muddling along up the street to an overdue bedtime.

He turned from the window and rubbed his eyes; and when he opened them again they lighted on the bottle. He sniffed again, stepped forward, picked it up and lobbed it across to Jo's bed. He slapped the envelope on his bedside table and flung himself down, full-length, face in pillow.

It was several moments before he turned, rolled on to his back and reached out to fumble for the envelope. He found it, held it high above his head and slowly thumbed it open. He pulled out the card.

On the front was a joke about a penguin that he didn't understand, and inside, in young, round, careful writing, was:

"I'm sorry if I get up your nose. But I'm glad you're my Dad, because I think you've got a good nose and I've inherited it. I don't mean to be a pain, and I hope you have a very HAPPY BIRTHDAY and I hope the bottle helps. But don't thank me too much, because you bought it for yourself really because I bought it with my pocket money which you give me. Ah well. That's life. Thanks for giving it to me - life, that is - and I'm sorry. Best wishes for today and everything. Jo."

His dad wanted to be irritated by the stupid jokiness, the clumsy repetitions. He made the irritation come. He chucked the card after the bottle, screwed the envelope into a ball and hurled it towards the pink rubbish bin with the flowery print on the side. He missed.

Snatching up the remote control he flicked on the television, perched on a bracket high on the wall, and a roar of noise and hectoring commentary blew back across the room.

"Oh, that's a great goal! That's a wonderful goal!"

"What, already?" he fumed aloud. "In August?"

He dabbed and squeezed at the channel buttons, but the damned thing wouldn't change.

"You'll not see a better volley than that! Sweet as you like! And you have to say the goal's been coming. Just look at this!"

Jo's dad responded, and watched the action replay. A ball was swung over from the left wing, and a young man, rising to meet it, turning slightly in the air and striking the very middle, sent it arrowing into the top corner.

"That is some goal!"

A second replay, from a different angle, at a different speed. In slow motion now; and something in the young man's shape, his flopping hair and slender waist, and the way he waved in celebration, reminded him of an afternoon in the park when he had stood, bored, between two coats, trying to be a goalkeeper as Jo, aping all his hero's mannerisms, fired goal after elegant goal.

"*Come on, Dad!*" Jo had called with a huge grin. "*You're too easy!*"

Pirouetting like a ballet dancer, flicking back that annoying lock.

"*No,* **it**'*s too easy!*" That's what he'd replied. "*Anyone can score with no defenders. And look at you. You'd be eaten alive on a rugby pitch. Try a proper contact sport.*"

"*Rugby's for the brainless,*" Jo had said, his face fallen.

"*And this game's for -* "

He switched off the memory, and flicked off the shots of the bacchic crowd. The screen went grey, and he tossed the remote control aside and lay back on the bed, staring at the ceiling in empty silence.

* * *

There was silence on the mound between Jo and Annie. He was afraid he'd killed all conversation by defending his dad. It crossed his mind to talk about her university, her course, or where she came from, and was plucking up the courage to ask if this was going to be her holiday when she beat him to it.

"Got any brothers or sisters?" she suddenly asked.

"Mmm? Oh. Yeah. Kate. My sister."

"Older than you?"

"No, no," said Jo. "Much younger, actually. Only a year."

"Nice?"

"Yeah," he said. "Yeah." And he brushed his hand along a fern. "Yeah. Really nice. She makes me laugh."

"Why, what does she do?"

He thought about it. "I don't know really. It's the way she is with Mum."

Annie waited, not wanting to have to keep prompting. But: "What about it?" she had to ask.

"Well...they just seem sort of...part of each other," Jo said, struggling to describe it. "Like, when she's feeding her."

"Well, she'll have done the same for you!" said Annie with a smile, but Jo wasn't listening: he was lost in the image.

"And when they're playing together," he said, "it's like she knows exactly what Mum's thinking: she's only got to look at her and she smiles and smacks her hands and stuff." He suddenly looked across at Annie and blushed. "Sorry, that sounds really stupid."

"No it doesn't," she said, but her mouth was twitching and he was sure she was laughing at him, and he looked down and started scratching at the earth again. "But you shouldn't imagine you were any different," she said again.

"What d'you mean?"

"She'll have been the same with you," said Annie. Jo threw a chalky pebble into the shadows. "Won't she?"

"Dunno," he muttered, with an inflection that made it clear he'd had enough. "Maybe."

There was a ragged flap of wings and a pigeon shuttled overhead. Jo looked up and followed its flight with a wistful gaze, as if it were the last bird he would ever see. And Annie watched him, and when the pigeon had disappeared from view she saw Jo hang his head. She reached into a shoulder bag sitting at her side, and opened a Bounty bar and gave him a piece.

"Good, these," she said. "Made for sharing - two separate bars in one pack."

"Mmm," said Jo, and they both took a big, moist bite.

"Only trouble is," she said a few moments later, "the coconut gets stuck in your teeth. Excuse me for being gross." And she picked at the space between canine and first molar. "I've got an awful food-trap here. God my nails are filthy. Ah. Gotcha." The coconut came out and she ate it. "I meant to buy plain but I got milk instead. Which do you prefer?"

Jo wasn't that bothered to be honest, but he made an effort, and soon they were on to the hoary topics of whether king-size bars were just *too* big, and whether chocolate was overpriced if shops could afford special offers of five for the price of three.

"I shouldn't eat any at all," said Annie. "Not with my figure."

"You're not fat," said Jo.

"Been looking, have you?" Jo glanced up and saw Annie grinning at him. He flushed, and tried to laugh it off. "No!" he said lamely, and turned his eyes away.

"Oh." She feigned disappointment. "I'm offended! But you've got to admit I fill this t-shirt."

He turned back, and saw that she was tugging it down - making it even tighter. He shuffled and cleared his throat. She gave a smile, and bit her lip, and said softly:

"What d'you think of the logo?"

Jo looked, as briefly as possible. He assumed the t-shirt's slogan was a joke, but he didn't get it. He was about to feign a grin when he saw her eyes. She was looking at him - in a way he'd not seen in a girl before. He went hot and cold and sat rigid, as if he'd been caught doing something wrong.

There was a pause; then she sighed, lay back, legs crossed at the ankle, arms pillowing her head, and shut her eyes.

Everything was very still. A crow cawed, and another answered. Jo looked at Annie again - then round at the trees. There was no scent, he noticed, not even of grass: the whole mound was covered with ivy and nightshade, or clumps of tall nettles, mottled with cow parsley, greying now.

"Once," Annie suddenly said, her eyes still shut, "this would all have been white. Amazing thought, isn't it? When they first built it, it would have been dazzling white chalk - you'd've seen it for miles. Same with all the burial mounds, and Silbury Hill, of course."

She yawned, stretched, and curled into a foetal position.

"Amazing," she said, dreamily. "Gleaming white amid all the green."

Again a crow cawed. Somewhere, a little way away, a car changed gear at a corner. There was no wind, and the air was dark and heavy. Jo looked yet again at Annie. Her lashes were very black with mascara, but her lips were pale, with no make-up.

He moved across to the tunnel.

He ran his hand gently around the mouth, feeling the damp, crumbly chalk; then he leaned slowly right into the darkness. He breathed in deeply, and closed his eyes. Down there, deep, deep down, in Merlin's mythical resting-place, they would send a camera to scan the mound's secrets, and then they would remove whatever was precious. And Gareth and Mort were defending it. It was all very -

Suddenly something brushed his cheek, his lip, his eye, and he scrambled back, beating it from his face. It caught in his hair, then flapped in a clumsy hover before vanishing into shadow. A moth.

Jo sighed, ruffled his hair, and looked at his watch. He tutted. It was much too early: nothing would happen yet. Maybe he could slip out of the hotel later and join his dad's shift at eleven. He could say he couldn't sleep and wanted to help. If his dad sent him back he could hide nearby and wait for the alarm. Hanging around now was –

"Hey!"

But suddenly everything changed.

"What's happened?" It was Annie's voice. He turned to see her sitting up. "The lamps have gone out."

It was really very dark, and Jo's eyes struggled to adjust. He took a pencil torch from his pocket and focused its tight, bright beam on the arc-lamps.

"Oh damn it," said Annie, "I haven't got a clue how to - " She stopped, listening intently. "Did you hear that?"

"What?"

"A bike."

"A motorbike?" said Jo.

"No, a bike. I thought I heard a bicycle bell."

They stood together, listening. In the distance they heard a car or two, slowing down to turn past the church. A dog barked, and someone called out and laughed, but nowhere near the mound. Then:

"There!"

Jo heard it, too - a playful ting of a bicycle bell, not far away.

"Oh, it's nothing," said Annie. "It'll just be the security bloke."

But looking at her, Jo knew she wasn't sure.

"I'll go and check," he said. "You stay here and watch the tunnel."

"Okay."

He switched off his torch and shuffled softly down the slope. He hopped on to the path at the bottom. Round the curving foot of the mound he crept, expecting at any second to see the shape of Gareth or Mort outlined against the College buildings. Somewhere nearby a generator hummed, powering a huge refrigerator in the refectory block. There was a rancid smell of wheelybins, all the worse because they were empty and their lids left open. Then, a few yards further on, he heard another sound: the pained creaking of a rusty hinge. He realised suddenly that he was near the strange folly he'd found before: the shell-lined grotto with the wrought iron gates. They were in there, he was sure of it.

"Mort," he called softly. "Gareth. It's me - Jo."

No reply. He crept closer.

And there, propped against the ornamental bars of the grotto's gates, was his bike: the bike he'd hired and left by the hawthorn tree at Silbury. God, he thought, why hadn't he gone back for it: the bloke in the hire place must've thought he'd -

There was something stuck on the saddle.

Jo looked all round, then took another step forward. He stopped again, and glanced behind him; then he walked slowly up to the bike. What he'd seen on the saddle was a scrap of paper, fixed with a gobbet of chewing gum. Jo pulled it off and the middle

61

ripped, but it was still legible. In hard, dark pencil, in surprisingly beautiful writing, were the words:

"Don't let your father do it, Jo. You must stop him."

A cold ripple down the back of his neck. He spun round, sure he was being watched. He flashed on his torch and panned it around… but there was no-one there. Nothing was moving, not even the leaves. Then he looked down, and noticed the bike's tyres were still deflated. So no-one had ridden it here: it meant they must have brought it on their -

"Ah!"

He blurted the cry and staggered back. A face in the grotto, inches from him, staring at him through the bars. Jo went white, the hairs on his neck erect and frozen. The face's mouth and eyes were appalled and gaping, like the tragic mask of a Cassandra, and the woman he had seen before slowly pushed the gates open, toppling the bike, and stood in the doorway staring straight at Jo. The head tipped to one side as she sank to her knees and stretched her arms wide in a pitiful plea. For the second time, Jo yelled and ran from her.

* * *

"Ye-e-e-s!!! Brilliant!"

Like football fans saluting a goal, the team of archaeologists punched the air and even exchanged a hug or two. The system was up and running, the first picture flowering into focus on their monitor screen. The camera, fitted with its own sharp light, was probing the tunnel, sending back instant images of the mound's inner body.

"Someone get the umbrella," said Jo's dad with his usual efficiency, and Annie heaved it open and shaded the screen from the bright morning sun.

There was a long pause. Everyone stared. It wasn't easy to manoeuvre the robot camera. On its caterpillar tracks it slid and

62

blundered. But what it showed was perfect: perfect whiteness; the tunnel, sloping diagonally down towards the mound's base, had been smoothly bored through carved chalk blocks. But then, a few moments later, it showed rougher surrounding walls and floor and ceiling.

"Chalk rubble," said Dave with instant authority; and he cleared his squeaky throat before explaining: "They built the mound with uncemented chalk blocks for the radial and concentric elements, and packed the interstices with small-grade chalk rubble."

Jo looked at him. Did *all* archaeologists talk like that?

"There'll be more blocks in a second," Dave said, and scratched his beard and tugged at his jumper rather nervously, then turned to the others and *da-dah*'d a mock-fanfare as the next picture reverted to a smooth-walled shaft.

"How far in do you think we are?" someone asked him.

"Give us a chance."

The robot lumbered on.

After a moment the same voice asked: "Who made this tunnel?"

"There are no records of prior digging," said Jo's dad. "At least, not to any depth."

"So - ?"

"Don't know."

"Could be medieval," someone else ventured. "You know - to do with the castle."

Jo's dad scoffed. "Can you honestly see John and his men digging something as perfect as this? It's almost wide enough to crawl down, but there's not a support to be seen."

"John?" Jo whispered to Annie, as the others huddled even closer to the screen.

"*King* John," she whispered back. "He had a huge castle here: incredibly important, actually - one of the strongest in all England. Used this mound as its motte, built a keep at the top. He was married here in fact - in a chapel that stood where those birch trees are: see? Had his treasury here, too. And went hunting up there in the Savernake Forest." She pointed towards the hills to the east.

"What," said Jo, "you mean *the* King John?"

"Well there's only been one! Feared by the good, loved by the bad. Stole from the poor, gave to himself. Taxed 'em rotten apparently. Nice man - got rid of his wife 'cause she couldn't give him a son, and bumped off his nephew to get the throne: Prince Arthur."

"Arthur?"

"Yeah, funny thought, isn't it? If it hadn't been for John there'd have actually been a King Arthur! Hello - what's happened?"

Dave was swearing. He'd stopped the robot. The picture was going fuzzy.

"Oh for God's sake," he cursed.

The picture had gone black. Then it flashed back up, a sheet of white.

"Come on, damn it."

Black again. And this time it stayed black. Dave thumped at the controls as the team all huffed and tutted. Then: "What the hell's that?"

The picture was slowly coming back. Up on the screen something strange was evolving: a weird swirl, something stirring in the shadows beyond the range of the camera's light.

"Focus," said Jo's dad, tense and agitated.

"D'you think I'm not trying?" said Dave. "Ah. Got it. We're back in business." But there was nothing to be seen. "Hmm. I think," he said, and scratched his beard, "it's finding it hard just to focus on the dark. I won't try and look ahead: I'll keep it fixed on the wall."

The robot continued on its way, but there was almost no sense of movement now: all it showed them was yard after blank yard of chalk to one side, inches away, as it rolled on gently down and down.

"This'll make great television," someone said sardonically, and a couple of others laughed.

"Just hold on, can't you?" Jo's dad snapped. "I reckon we're nearly there."

Another minute passed. It couldn't be much further now to the base of the Stone Age pile. Birds were busy overhead, and behind them traffic hummed and rumbled, but silence hung over the huddle at the screen. Whiteness. Pure whiteness. And then:

"It's stopped."

It had. Dave had done nothing to the controls, but the robot was definitely not moving.

"It must have reached the bottom! Turn the camera!" said Jo's dad. "See what's ahead!"

The team gazed at the screen, wide-eyed. As the camera slowly turned, the picture changed from near-featureless white to shapeless shadow.

"Focus! Focus!"

The swirl of blur became clear and sharp, but made no sense. The camera panned to right and left, trying to get a sense of size.

Then it did. And it was absurd.

What they seemed to be looking at, in extreme close-up, was a dank, matted beard.

"Pull back! Come on! Come on!"

A flutter at the controls and the camera was in reverse.

"Stop! Now what's that?"

They were all expecting a staring head. None of them would have admitted it but, for all their rational training, that beard had conjured visions of a buried Merlin. But as it now came into focus it revealed itself to be not hair but - somewhat bewilderingly - grass. The gardeners among them were reminded of the times they'd bought rolls of turf for an instant lawn, and unravelled them to find a damp, dull, flattened mat. They stared, uncomprehending. And there, nestling in this peaty mass of turf and moss, was something small and black.

"What's that?" It was Jo's dad speaking. "Move in, slowly."

The camera crept forward, and after looking for a breathless moment, Dave said: "It's an ant."

"But it's got wings."

"A flying ant."

"Is it alive?"

"No."

"What's it doing there?"

"I'd say it was buried with the grass," said Dave.

"What d'you mean?"

"I mean it's a Stone Age ant."

Someone laughed, but Dave continued: "Under Silbury they found a mound of turf, with insects preserved in it. This is the same. If it's a flying ant, it means the turf mound was made around this time of year - late July or early August."

"You mean," said Annie, "they built these gigantic monuments over mounds of turf?"

"Yeah."

Then Jo added: "I thought you said they found nothing at Silbury."

Jo's dad was startled to hear Jo speak; in fact he'd forgotten Jo was there. He said: "That's right."

"But Dave just said - "

"They found grass and insects."

"That's not nothing," said Jo.

"Oh for God's sake. We're talking about a *real* find. Look," his dad said quickly, turning back to Dave, "how can the ant be so well preserved?"

Dave shrugged. Then he froze, and then looked up at Jo's dad. Annie gasped. And suddenly, Jo had the sense that an idea had visited everyone's mind at the very same instant: if something - or someone - were *under* that turf, they'd surely be as perfectly preserved as -

"This is fantastic!" Jo's dad cried; and patting the ground on the mound's steep flank he said: "Brace yourself for some serious digging - we're coming in!"

There was a strange growling cheer from the team. But:

"Don't let your father do it, Jo...You must stop him..."

All Jo could think of was the note... and the Cassandra mask... and the woman's outstretched hands, pleading...

Oh, it was ridiculous: how could he possibly stop the dig? What had it to do with him? Suddenly, overwhelmingly, Jo just wanted to run away - from the dig, from Marlborough, from everything. He scrambled up a bank of ivy, braved nettle and bramble and clambered swiftly up the mound. He'd made no decision to do this: his limbs just took him and he kept on going.

6. The Castle

*I*n moments he had reached the top; but what he saw there was wholly unexpected. The glorious calm of Silbury's grassy, open crown was not a feature of this Marlborough mound. There was no view offered in any direction: the trees, strained and wizened descendants of the spiral planted centuries ago, continued right to the brow, encircling it completely; and new ones, too, had been planted on the top - and almost all were funereal yew, radiating the gloom of a municipal graveyard. And if he'd thought to find remains of King John's keep he was mistaken. Not even foundation stones; the only structure was a tall brick chimney, bizarrely unconnected to anything, shrouded by trees, festooned with graffiti and looming pointlessly. Where the keep had stood a colossal hole had been gouged, ten feet deep and thirty feet wide, a blind socket stuffed with weeds and brambles; and in the middle of this wretched hole, planted on a concrete base and stained all round with dreary algae, was a massive rectangular tank made of bolted metal plates - an enormous cistern: the water-source for the scholarly establishment below.

Jo prowled around it, shaking his head. He tried to picture a castle keep, and wondered if it had been attacked, and how many souls had entered or had left the world in that very spot. But then he recalled that people didn't live in keeps: they were only for defence; they'd have lived - and given birth and passed away in sick-beds - in buildings down below: in the bailey, where Annie had said a chapel had stood, the marriage-place apparently of Robin Hood's great enemy King John.

Jo looked through a gap in the trees and down to the mound's foot - to the bailey. He could see his dad waving instructions to the team, and Dave in the rose garden, mobile on one ear, finger in the other, no doubt ordering the machines that would blunder through the chalk and the turf and plunder whatever lay beneath.

But how was he supposed to stop it? What could he possibly do?

"Oh, who cares?" he suddenly shouted; then muttered: "The mound's ruined already: look at it."

Jo wanted rescuing. He felt tired - tired and very alone - caught in the middle of something that couldn't possibly, he convinced himself, concern a fourteen-year-old.

But while a large part of him wanted no responsibility, there was another part - however much he might resist and deny it - that was curious, that wanted an explanation. If he wanted anyone to rescue him, it was the pair with the sidecar: he wanted them to carry him off to Dag on their motorsickle and let him into this mystery.

But he hardly knew that.

For the moment he sighed, turned away, walked past the cistern and the incongruous chimney and round to the opposite side.

A soiled sheet of a tabloid 'paper was stuck on a bramble. Grotesquely inflated mammary glands, long blond hair and high-heeled shoes... Jo pulled it from the thorns, looked swiftly and was about to rip it up when his eye caught the headline on the facing page. His favourite player wanted a move: he wouldn't sign a new contract. It was outrageous! This man *was* the team: he'd been with the club from the youth team upwards. But now, it seemed, it wasn't good enough. He wanted Champions League football, the column said, and more money in a week than the Prime Minister earned in a year. The club was unlikely to qualify and couldn't possibly meet his wage demands, so now he was off to Spain. "Just like that," Jo muttered. "But I stick with them." Through thick and thin. Mainly thin. So what was he supporting? A team? Or a bunch of men on contracts? It was as sordid as the page three girl. He screwed the sheet into a lumpy ball and punted it right-footed off the mound.

As he watched it fly through a gap in the trees his eye fell on a different excavation down below: foundations were being dug for a new College building, but all work seemed to have stopped despite the summer weather. There was just one man in a hard-hat and boiler suit, standing motionless at the edge of the fenced-off site. For no particular reason Jo stood and watched him for the best part of a minute; but all the man did was take off his hard-hat, mop his bald head with a handkerchief and stand staring at nothing. Suddenly Jo had had enough of the mound. He saw the top of the concrete steps that offered a short cut down. He went straight over, and made his way to the foot.

As he neared the bottom Jo pulled up sharply: the man in the hard-hat was sitting on the last step. He was very slowly wiping the back of his neck. Jo hopped to one side to get past him, and was conscious of the man looking at him as he walked on. It was ridiculous not to say hello, Jo thought: he might think I'm a snob. So he turned and nodded, awkwardly late though the acknowledgement was. The man nodded back. Jo walked on a short way, and stopped at the fence around the building site. The mechanical diggers had been at work all right - the soil had been ravaged over a huge area. But it was awash. In spite of the baking August heat the site was a mire of soaking mud. How ever could they build on ground so wet?

"Disaster," the man said, wandering up to Jo's shoulder. "Typical architects - you'd've thought they'd've found out before we started: we're building on a spring!"

"A spring?"

"Yeah! There's a spring down there that used to feed the castle moat, and we can't stop it! You've got to laugh!"

And he turned and trudged away with a rueful chuckle.

A hot wind struck up and stirred the trees. The sun was dazzlingly bright. As Jo squinted through the glare he noticed ahead of him, on the high green ridge that rose beyond the river, a giant white horse - not a real one, but an elegant, noble picture cut into the turf.

"Ride a cock horse to Banbury Cross - "

From nowhere his mum's voice came into his head, singing his sister Kate to sleep.

" - See a fine lady on a white horse..."

Jo hoofed the memory away with a flailing kick at the gravel. Then he sighed, and he slumped, and he stood, lost and aimless, looking back through the fence at the building site, a lake of chaotic mud.

And then, as he stared, he found himself suddenly unable to focus. Then he was dazzled - dazzled by the sun, searing, blinding off a sheet of water; for it seemed to him that water was oozing across the jumble of tyre-tracks, rising and spreading at alarming speed into a shimmering pool. He shook his head and rubbed his eyes to soothe their shock, and then, when he looked again -

"Ah!"

- the fence and the building-site were gone: they had simply vanished. In their place, and right before him, was a shining fountain; and in its centre, embracing herself to hide her nakedness, stood a young woman, shuddering with cold... and terror. For toward her, mounted on a great black horse, rode a knight, heavy, iron-clad, savage, lowering his lance and darkly crying:

"Maiden, this place is mine now!"

She turned her face to Jo, desperate, pleading.

"You can see what's happening!" she cried. "Save me, boy!"

Jo stared back, aghast and baffled, as the knight's horse plashed its hooves in the water and the knight's lance plunged into the maiden's chest. The lance-head burst from her back with a brilliant gush of rich, red blood. Her body lurched in a single convulsion and hung, skewered, on the ashwood shaft. The knight swung from his saddle, tipped the lance on end to drop the body in the water, and dug his boot in her stomach as he heaved his weapon from her flesh.

"No!"

It was Jo's own voice yelling. The knight looked up and turned towards him.

"What is it, boy?" The voice snarled hollow inside the helmet. Jo stood, gasping for air. "What is it? The maiden's dead and I shall have this place. Her body will be buried in the foundations."

Jo turned to run, but before he understood what was happening he heard the knight's horse whinny, hooves beating turf, and turned to see the beast, eyes crazed and mindless, rearing above him and about to deliver two hammer-blows.

* * *

When Jo awoke and shifted his back, he found he was lying on straw. A thin grey light was slanting on to a damp stone wall, and stone walls, he saw, surrounded him. The ceiling was stone, and the floor beneath the straw was stone. The door was oak and iron. He heaved himself to his feet, and looked up through the high barred window. There was thick fog outside, and it was bitterly cold. He stumbled to the door and beat on it.

"Hello!"

He beat again, several times.

"Hello!"

No sound came, either from beyond the door or from beyond the window. But from inside his chest, he realised, came rapid, gasping breaths, and he fought to control himself. He hugged himself tightly - as, he recalled, the maiden in the fountain had done - and strode around the tiny cell, kicking the straw in rising panic. Back to the door he went and beat again.

"Who's out there? Open up! Open up!"

He wasn't going to cry; it was all too ridiculous. And then he yelled the most unexpected thing:

"Mum! Mum!"

Of all people, the mother he hadn't seen for months was the least likely to appear. Would *anyone*? Did anyone exist in this strange new place?

"Where the hell *am* I? Mum…"

He gulped back a sob, then heaved in great breaths, his feet spread apart, his back against the door. And then...footsteps. Approaching footsteps. He stopped his panting, and stood stock still. The footsteps halted. Any moment now a key would turn the lock.

But no sound came.

"Hello! Please open! Is there anybody there?"

Still no key. Were the footsteps moving away? He turned and put his mouth to the keyhole, cold and rusty against his lips.

"Please! Please open up!"

Not a sound.

"Please!" And then Jo stopped, frozen: he was suddenly aware of a presence behind him. Inside the room.

He didn't dare to look. Because he knew who it was. There was no word spoken, but Jo knew exactly what was being said. He had to be brave. He closed his eyes, and turned, and faced her.

And when he opened his eyes, he was nearly blinded by the light from the vessel that she held. Her face was just a shadow beyond that light, but he looked into the space that was framed by her hair and saw, first, the woman who had squatted to give birth in the grotto, then the lady in the water when he fell from Silbury, then the maiden who had pleaded for his help in the fountain. As one face melted gently into the next, she nodded towards the vessel, a deep, open bowl. And as Jo gazed into its dazzling light, he knew that he was safe and that rescue would come.

"Can I keep it?" he said softly, but he knew the answer was no, that it was his to find in the future, but that while it was with him it would give him all the food and comfort that he craved. For several minutes, so it seemed, he bathed in its warmth and radiance; then it melted away, and he was alone again.

Then noise down below, outside, and a scraping clatter just beyond the window. Jo scrambled across and ducked down below the sill, and moments later a face in a chain-mail hood appeared above him at the bars.

"Joel," the voice called softly. "Joel, are you there, boy?"

He knew the voice, but couldn't place it. Then another voice, familiar also, gave a whispered call from further off:

"Is he not there?"

"Joel?"

He could tell the voices meant him no harm. They were concerned, intending help.

"Joel?"

He called back: "Yes. I'm here." And he stood up and looked into the face. Again it seemed familiar, but he had to be mistaken, for peering through the bars was a knight in chain mail, the top of a heraldic surcoat just visible above the window ledge.

"We're come to rescue you."

A moment later the knight was tying a rope around two of the window's wooden bars. When he was certain all was secure he turned and gestured to the one behind him, and Jo could faintly hear a horse's snort and an awkward thudding of hooves. He saw the rope go taut; then it creaked and strained; the knots in the rope went tighter still; then with a weird, un-wooden ripping the bars transformed to gawky teeth as the rope burst away and left them a broken, twisted mess.

"Is there a gap enough?" said the knight. "You're a good, broad lad!"

"I'll try!"

And Jo reached high and grabbed the sill and heaved himself

into the window space. His feet could find no purchase on the smooth, damp wall of the cell, but the strength in his arms was enough to drag him up and on to the wooden teeth. He paused there a moment, half in, half out, taking breath.

"Well done, Joel," said the knight. "Now give me your hand and I'll pull you through."

"I don't think I'll do it," said Jo. "It's going to be too tight. You should've taken out *three* bars."

"Your shoulders are through," the knight replied. "Unless you're a most uncommon shape you'll make it!"

Jo smiled, and thrust out a hand. The knight took it, and pulled with surprising strength. But as Jo emerged and straddled the sill he gasped with a sudden giddy fear at the drop that yawned beneath him: the knight was perched on a wooden ladder long enough to scale a castle wall - absurdly long, it seemed to Jo; but he felt compelled to show no fear, and with only one hand clutching a bar he swung his feet out and paddled in thin air, feeling for a rung. The knight took hold of one ankle and set his foot firmly on the first strut; Jo, amazed by his own mad courage, felt perfect balance and confidence as he grasped the ladder's sides and began to clamber down.

Soon his feet padded plump on soft turf, and he turned to see a second mail-hooded face smiling at him, as bafflingly familiar as his first rescuer's; and they were both beckoning him towards a short grey pony that stood solemnly beside their larger mounts. Jo had never ridden in his life, but didn't want to admit it. Instead he said:

"What about the ladder?"

They shook their heads and indicated silence; so Jo took another deep breath, stepped forward and, trying to remember what he'd seen in films, put a foot in a stirrup and swung on to the pony's back. It felt quite convincing. Then they set off into the fog.

It was a dense mass of tiny droplets, thick, cold and wet in the lungs. As they rode, the only sound beyond their hooves was the heavy dripping of the lank, bare trees. Not a bird in the air, not a rustle in the grass. Jo's pony gave a sneeze-like snort, and shook his head repeatedly. Jo's trust was total: much greater than any misgiving was his certainty that he knew these men, these tall, mail-clad shapes that jogged before him and led him...where?

"Where are we going?" he asked.

One of the knights turned and pointed straight ahead.

"Cardoil," he replied, with a smile that suggested Jo should be pleased.

And they carried on at a measured walk through a wasteland.

On either side of the muddy track were fields, but they were dismal: as the fog slowly lifted, Jo saw nothing growing but tussocks of thistle in a wretched scrub of grass and chickweed; and here and there lay the long-dead, crow-pecked carcasses of cattle.

After a long, plodding ride they crested a low ridge, and Jo saw ahead, in the shallow valley of a drab river, the battlemented walls of a small city. Banners hung limp from place to place, and columns of hearth-smoke meandered skyward.

On they rode until at last they neared the gate, but not before they had passed through a shanty town of crumbling cob. Wattle-and-daub walls were disintegrating with damp, children coughing consumptively, and dogs lay too lifeless to rummage in the stinking refuse. The knights' reaction was to place a languid hand over mouth and nose; Jo gaped in amazement.

"Pass on."

The gatekeeper sat slumped and waved them through without a glance, and their hooves clattered suddenly on cobbles, ringing loud under the gatehouse roof. Up a winding street they passed, but it was eerily devoid of sound or life. Shops were shuttered, doors shut tight. Then, some minutes later, they climbed down at a mounting-block outside a great stone hall. Up a flight of stairs Jo followed the knights; then they ushered him in.

Jo was astounded.

The hall, lit bright with fires and candles, was filled with knights and ladies, magnificently dressed in greens and scarlets, blues and golds, all seated at long tables as if waiting for a feast. And straight ahead, at a table set upon a long, low dais, sat a king: Jo knew this, not because of a crown or sceptre, for he had none, but partly by the splendour of the high, carved chair on which he sat, and mostly by his aura. This king looked up when the knights and Jo walked in; but it was only for a moment: evidently disappointed, he returned his bearded chin to where it had been propped in his hands. And so the hall sat, full and waiting.

The knights and Jo sat down together on a bench at one of the tables. And it was then, and only then, that the two knights, whom Jo had sensed so strongly that he knew, threw back the hoods of their mailcoats so that their faces could be fully seen. Still he couldn't place them.

Suddenly the silence was broken by a tinkling of bells, and a figure came scrambling from beneath the king's table. He was dressed in a shambolic patchwork of leather scraps and padded stuff, and wisps of greasy hair stuck out from under his bell-tasselled cap. He lurched towards Jo and the knights, clapping his hands and laughing inanely. He was babbling:

"Here he is! Here he is! A saviour at last! A saviour!"

He was looking straight at Jo, and Jo yet again had the uncanny feeling that he had seen the face before. The fool looked round for a reaction from the crowded hall, but no-one was responding.

"I tell you true!" he cried. "This boy could be the one!"

Jo was still riffling through a mental album of faces from his recent past when the fool said something else, something that made it all fall into place:

"This boy's stupendous! He can see the past and see the gods. He's seen the Lady of the Lake!"

It was Dag. It was the nutter. And sure enough, he heard the king say: "Be quiet, Dagonet. Leave the boy be."

That unforgettably strange name again. And turning to glance at the knights who had rescued him, Jo realised why he had known their faces: it was Gareth and Morton, the motorsickle men. They understood his puzzlement, and as Dagonet chuckled back to his place at the king's foot, Gareth turned to Jo and said softly:

"You wonder, I know, how we can be here and there, in your time and in this time."

Jo thought about this, and nodded. Gareth smiled and, cupping a hand to his mouth as he leaned right up to Jo's ear, he whispered:

"You and I - and all people - are in our own world and at the same time, if we only knew it, in other worlds, too. We inhabit a different world for every person that we meet."

"Oh, but - " Jo started to whisper a protest, but Gareth put a finger to his lips.

"No," he said. "It's easy to deny this, but each of us sees a different world, and only one of many. And think of your dreams. How often do you wake and, remembering a dream, say: 'Where did that come from?' - as if it were not a part of you. But it is. And it comes from the world you inhabit daily, but don't know that it's there. Our dreams reveal our other life in our other worlds. And so do the stories that we tell. That is why people hunger for stories so. Stories are a necessity: they give us glimpses of our other worlds."

"But... they're not *real*," Jo said uncertainly.

"Of course they are. People make them up. They make them up because they're *there*."

Jo frowned. This was difficult - and surely nonsense. But somehow, he thought... And Mort was gently nodding agreement. Then Gareth spoke on in his calm, measured voice.

"Deep down we've always known this, though many now seem dead to it. And deep down we know the people - and the gods - in those other worlds. You know, do you not, exactly who that king is?"

"It's Arthur," Jo said without a moment's thought. "And this is his court. But I don't know why everyone's so still."

"We're waiting," said Gareth solemnly, and he turned to

survey the vaulted hall. "This feast cannot begin until a marvel appears - an adventure. But our king and all the court are languishing - so listless, so weary, that we wonder if they'd have the heart to meet an adventure's challenge."

And Morton, ever the one to ape a voice, became mock-mystical as he rolled his eyes and whispered: "Some marvel we need in this middle-earth!"

And with that, the hall returned to stillness. The only movement came from shadows cast by the fires; the only sound was the crackle of the hearth-logs; otherwise all was silent.

It was a silence so profound that everyone present was sharply aware, minutes later, of the sound that broke it.

At first far off, then nearer and nearer, came a single set of hoofbeats: someone was slowly riding - as Jo, Gareth and Morton had done - up the street towards the mounting-block. But whoever it was didn't stop to dismount. The hoofbeats continued, and soon were unmistakably making their heavy, ungainly way up the stone steps to the hall. Jo looked towards the king: he didn't stir, but around the hall Jo saw heads beginning to turn and eyes exchanging glances. The hooves had reached the top of the steps. And had stopped.

There was a long silence.

In one of the hall's hearths a log toppled with a crash and a shower of sparks. High up in the hammerbeam roof a startled bird flapped wildly from a rafter and swooped low over a table, causing a lady to cry out and flail at the air. It flew straight at a window and thudded into a bright blue pane, then wheeled back with mad beatings. A servant took it upon himself to usher the bird out. He heaved open the door and the bird flew free.

And there, looming in the entrance, huge and motionless, was an ox. And on the ox's back, saddleless but entirely poised, was mounted a woman, very tall, very lean and of astounding age. Her skin was shrunk so tight, her eyes sunk so deep, that Jo felt he was staring at a skull. Sparse strands of lifeless hair hung from her leathery pate, and her arms, as alarmingly thin as Jo had seen on the victims of some African famine, hung straight and dead by her sides. The knights and ladies gaped, aghast, wide-eyed. But when Jo looked to the top of the hall, he saw the king no longer slumped and listless but standing, alert and tense.

There was a long pause, and then:

"You are welcome here!" the king cried, and flung his arms wide.

With that the ox raised its head, crowned with a mighty moon of horn, and began to lumber forward, bringing its rider, erect and rigid, into the heart of the hall. When it reached the exact centre it stopped.

After a long moment, the woman's ancient head - and nothing else - began to move. It turned its gaze on everyone: no-one felt excluded. The fires in the hearths had died, and such light as remained in the hall was grey. And then, turning straight ahead to face the king, she slowly parted her shrunken lips and began to move her tongue. As if trying to rediscover speech, at first she made no sound. Then a straining breath; then, a gesture: she was raising her left hand; and as it began to turn with awful slowness in his direction, Jo knew with utter certainty that it would stop at him. It did. And at last, and very slowly, words came from the woman's head. This is what she said:

"That boy... That boy you saw fit to save... But you did not save *her*."

The king made no reply. He did not understand.

"Those knights beside him..." Her voice cracked on. "It was a simple matter, rescuing him from his cell... But to free the maiden from her burial-place would demand that castle's utter destruction... And who in this wretched court of yours has the heart to do that: to release her, and restore life to this wasteland? I tell you this: you have all seen the sacred vessel - what human ever born has not? - but you reverence it no longer. That boy was the last to behold its wonder, but has forgotten it already."

80

At this, Jo remembered the maiden-mother showing him the deep bowl and its dazzling light.

"He remembers now," the old woman was saying; and Jo realised that her eyes were fixed on him; and as he looked into her skull-like face he saw it blur into the maiden's, then the mother's; then she was the hag once more, and saying:

"And he it was who saw the maiden slaughtered. He was imprisoned by her murderer, and Gareth and Morton, seated there, while nobly seeking the sacred vessel, learned of the boy's plight and went to rescue him. All well and good. But until the maiden is saved from where she lies entombed in stone, and until she is held in proper reverence, the vessel's light will be denied to all and the wasteland will remain."

There was no response from the king, from anyone. With an exhalation that was half sigh, half snort of contempt, the old, old woman nudged the ox's flanks, and the beast turned slowly and tramped back to the door. The servant hauled it open again, and in their own time the ox and its ancient rider were gone.

As soon as the door was shut tight once more, servants scurried to rekindle the fires; but the king stopped them with a shout, saying:

"No!" and his voice echoed hollow in the hall. "How can we think of comfort? We've been presented with a marvel now, an adventure; but it signals not a feast but a feat. The goddess has laid down a challenge. Who dares meet it?"

"It's the strongest castle ever seen," said Gareth.

"Defended by the mightiest companies," said Mort.

"Do you then not have the heart for this?" the king asked.

"What do *you* say, Jo?"

The question came from far away.

"Jo? What do you say?"

He looked from side to side, confused.

"Jo?" the voice said again. It was a girl's voice, not a knight's. "Jo! For God's sake!"

And a hand was on his shoulder, shaking him. It was Annie in her jeans and t-shirt, her other hand shading her eyes from the dazzling sun.

"God, Jo, where *are* you?" she said, half-laughing. "You look completely out of it!"

"Oh," he grunted, looking round bewildered, trying to get his bearings. Then he saw the razor-wire fence and the mud-filled building site. "Oh. Yeah. Sorry."

"Under-age drinking, is it?" she said, nudging him. "Shame!"

Jo did his best to find a laugh. He managed an awkward smile.

"Anyway, did you hear what I said? We're taking a break and going up the forest - the Savernake Forest. The giant digger Dave's ordered won't be here till tomorrow, so there's nothing we can do for a bit. Your dad said you might like to come."

"Yeah. Yeah, sure." Jo tried to clear his throat. His voice was croaky, as if he'd been running through fog.

"Don's gone to buy some sarnies and stuff," said Annie, as they started to walk back towards the dig. "We'll have a good old-fashioned picnic." She smiled. "But drink strictly for eighteens and up!"

7. The Forest

"**O**n my head, Jo! Oh, well done, my son! And the goalkeeper has *no* chance!"

In spite of the heat a boisterous football match was under way, with the usual running commentary. The clearing was a perfect size for a five-a-side, and the Forestry Commission had thoughtfully provided tables and benches for picnicking spectators, with litter bins prominently close - toilets, too - even barbecues for the entirely organised; and every effortless convenience was marked with internationally recognisable, matchstick-people signs.

Jo took the ball on his left foot, switched it to his right and was about to let fly when bearded, barrel-chested Dave - still, incredibly, wearing a jumper - came thundering in from behind. Jo's lungs emptied as he hit the ground, and a great cry went up:

"Oh, ref! He took him out!"

From the picnic tables came female laughter. It was all good, extrovert male fun, the student dig-assistants - especially lanky Richie and shaven-headed Don - flirting madly with Annie and her other t-shirted mates. Jo said nothing. He couldn't match the archaeology students for size - and he wasn't yet ready for flirting - but he could show them up for skill, and he brushed himself down, picked up the ball and prepared to take a free kick. Just a three-step run-up from a steep angle, then he whipped his foot round the outside of the ball and watched it swerve wickedly past a bewildered 'keeper and into what would have been the top corner if they'd had anything more than coats for posts.

"It's there!" yelled prime commentator Don. "5-4! What a goal by the youngster on his début!"

"No way!" said Richie in goal. "Well over!"

"What colour is the sky in your world?" said Don. "In off the bar!"

"What does the Russian linesman say?"

Jo was having no part in this. He was jogging into the trees to retrieve the ball. It had gone a fair way, and come to rest in some drab undergrowth just beyond the clearing's edge. He stepped in and picked it up, and found it smeared with the dog's mess that was everywhere. By the time he'd wiped it off in some long grass, and made his way back to the pitch, the players were drifting back to the picnic tables and the plastic party-size bottles of beer and the carrier bags of supermarket sandwiches. Jo felt completely out of place, nearly a decade younger than anyone else, and he rolled the ball in their direction, turned away and went into the trees.

He wandered very slowly for a minute or two, observing the shapes of old, dead tree trunks, gnarled and knotted, the fabulous patterns of light and shadow, the amazing array of different greens. It was beautiful – he knew that's what he was supposed to think. And, yes, he could see that. But it was strange: he didn't quite feel that he was *there*, that he was a part of it. Maybe his dad was right - he spent too long in front of screens, or seeing the world from the glass cocoon of a moving car, flashing past like just another film. He took a long blink and then tried to see anew, to look at the forest as if his eyes were *not* a camera, tried to sense himself as an animal, as much a part of the living world as the sapling by his knee. He reached out and touched it, trying to *connect*. It was tough, springy – certain, it seemed to Jo, of its right to be in the world. Some of its leaves were disfigured by grubs; others were brown and curling with disease. But it would survive. Jo sensed that even if it were cropped to its base it would spring back all the fiercer: the life in its roots would never be denied. So why did Jo doubt his *own* right to be there? Why was he always so awkward and embarrassed? He took a deep breath and stood up tall.

Then he went hot and cold.

Sitting on a tree-stump, breast-feeding a baby, was a woman with the hair and figure of his mother. He couldn't breathe. But then he saw the baby was too young to be Kate, and the woman's rumpled top was a colour his mum would never have worn. She hadn't seen Jo, so there was no need for a blush or an apology. He pushed aside a low branch and crunched away, sweating, over leaves and beech-mast.

Almost immediately he stumbled on to a neat tarmac road. There wasn't much mystery to these woods, he thought; none at all when he saw a smart, prefabricated warden's cabin, and a telephone booth beside it.

But suddenly the telephone interested him. It was obvious who he needed to call, who he needed to speak to. He patted his pocket and felt a few coins, checked inside and found what he needed. But would she want him to call? Did she prefer it without him, like his dad said? Would she ever want to see him again? Would his voice be an unnecessary pain? He swallowed hard, and licked his lips. Then he walked up and struggled with the door, and pulled it stiffly shut behind him. The booth stank of cigarette smoke, and the receiver was a yellowing grey with grime, but he plonked in the coins and dialled. No reply at first. Then an electronic bleep and a hiss like the prelude to an answerphone, then what sounded like breathing at the other end.

"Hello?" said Jo, uncertainly. "Hello... Mum?"

No reply.

"Kate? Kate, if that's you, can you put it down and call Mum?"

What was he saying? Kate wasn't old enough to understand. He called again, louder this time:

"Mum, are you there?"

A pause, then a sound like a sigh, a sad sigh.

"Mum... Is that you, Mum? Please answer."

Was the sound that followed a sob?

"... Mum, I really want to talk to - "

Click. Bleep. "I'm sorry I'm not here to take your call," came his mother's recorded voice, "but if you leave your name and number, and any message you may have, I'll call you back as soon as I can. Thank you. Please wait for the tone."

There was an appalling wailing whistle like feedback, making Jo recoil; then the briefest blip. Was that the recording tone? Surely not. Jo hesitated, uncertain whether to speak or not; and as he stood, inhibited, it struck him that he had no idea what to say. How could he leave a message about the things he'd seen? How could she possibly understand? He hung up the receiver and turned round.

He reeled back with a cry.

Staring at him through the door, his face pressed almost to the glass, was an enormous figure, helmeted, cloaked and wielding a spear. There was another behind him, and another. The man raised his spear, and Jo stood rooted in terror. Then the man turned to the right and started to prowl behind the booth. The others followed him, spears ready. Then a hand landed on Jo's shoulder, and as he made to scream a second hand clapped his mouth.

"It isn't you they're looking for," breathed a deep male voice in his ear.

And suddenly it wasn't glass in front of him: it was wood. And the only light was trickling through a tiny crack at eye level, and filtering down from a hole high overhead. He was inside the trunk of a hollow tree.

"Let them move on," the voice murmured. "They haven't the patience."

A minute passed, a minute in which Jo breathed deep and steady, trying to keep control until he could turn and see his captor...or was it his protector? Neither the smell nor the touch of

86

this man gave him any sense of danger, and the tree's heart was warm and eternally secure.

At last the man released his hold - and the strangest of things happened: they were suddenly - and Jo had no idea how - outside the tree. And they were surrounded by deep, gaunt winter forest and standing in thick snow.

"They saw my footprints," said the man with a smile, "but they can never fathom how I pass into wood."

He was of no great height and of indeterminate age. Against the dark winter trunks he was brown, invisible; but Jo knew, as though he had always known it, that this man was underlyingly green.

The man took a few steps ahead, stooping a little, his eyes scanning the pattern of prints in the snow; then he nodded, satisfied.

"They've gone," he said. "Back to their horses, back to the castle." He turned to look at Jo for the first time. "But what brings *you* here, boy? If you were armed I'd have said you were after the king's deer. Just gathering firewood? He's not even keen to allow *that*, you know: it's a dangerous game."

With that he cupped his hands to his mouth and gave a strange bird-call. And suddenly Jo was aware of other figures, dressed just like this man, appearing from the trees; and not from behind them or between them, but *from* them: it was as if, like ghosts walking through walls, they were emanating from the trunks. Their clothes and hair, their eyes, even their skin, were the colours of beech- and oak-bark, and each man carried a bow and quiver.

"If we're determined," the man, who was evidently their captain, said to them, "we can be there before nightfall. Keep off the main tracks, and make for the churchyard, underneath the yew."

In an instant, without a word, they started to melt into the dense brown wood; and the man turned to Jo and said, with real sympathy:

"Are you lost?"

Jo felt it an entirely apt description, and nodded.

"From Merleberg, are you?"

A pause while Jo made sense of the town's older, variant name, then he nodded again.

"Then come with me, boy, and I'll see you safe home."

With total trust Jo followed him, and together they creaked away through the snow.

* * *

By the time they reached the churchyard the sun was sinking, its last red streaks of light bloodying the snow. Jo felt a groan and a snap underfoot as he stepped on a frozen puddle, but the ice held; and he walked on with the captain and soon saw a huddle of shadows underneath an ancient yew. He recognised the outline of the church: they were at the eastern end of Marlborough. And although the roof-line that stretched away towards the low sun in the west was completely unfamiliar, the thatched timber buildings formed the shape of the gently curving, unusually wide High Street that Jo knew. And at the far end, where he expected to see the College with the mound hidden behind, he saw the towers and battlements of an immense stone castle.

"Well, boy," said the woodsmen's captain, "it's time for you to go. You know your way from here, I take it?"

"I thought I would," Jo said, "but, well, things have changed. Are you going to the castle?"

"After a fashion. You don't live *there*, do you?"

"No!" said Jo, sensing a 'yes' would earn the captain's instant enmity. "I just - "

But before Jo could take the awkward matter further, there was a sharp hiss from the yew tree, and everyone ducked low. Jo ducked with them. Along the road in the hollow below the churchyard a company of knights were riding, heading for the castle; and a train of packhorses followed behind, laden with the limp, flopping, antlered victims of a day's wild hunting.

"Dear God," murmured one of the captain's men. "How many do they need? There's half a herd on the backs of those ponies."

"They have big bellies in the castle," whispered another. "And the more you have, the more you want."

"But how fast do they think deer breed? Savernake may be plentiful, but they don't appear by magic."

"It's King John's favourite hunting ground," said the captain. "He'll do the same tomorrow, and the next day, and the next if the fancy takes him. Even this snow didn't put him off."

"Against the white the target's plainer."

"And meanwhile, my friends, *our* target's invisible," said the captain. "Imprisoned inside those castle walls."

"Do we know which tower her dungeon's in?" asked one of his men.

"The new," he replied, "the biggest, where the moat is deepest. They've built it since her capture, as if specially to keep her."

So that's why they're here, thought Jo. They've come to rescue a woman. But one of the captain's men was protesting:

"We'll never free her from there! It's impossible!"

There were several sombre grunts of agreement.

"If you're right," said the captain, "the greenwood's dead forever. Without the Maid, without Marian, we'll all be joyless, lifeless. We *have* to save her."

Marian? Jo started, wondering if he'd heard aright. Maid Marian? The greenwood? And he looked again at the green-brown figures in the shadow of the yew - the outlaws who'd appeared from the forest trees - and again at their captain who had saved him in the hollow trunk; and the question emerged and he hardly dared to ask it. But he did.

"Are you," he said, stumbling a little in his awe, "are you Robin - Robin Hood?"

"That's one of my names," the captain replied.

"But I thought you lived in *Sherwood* Forest - by Nottingham."

"I live in the wood," he said. "Barnsdale, Sherwood, Arden, Savernake, they are all one. From the Weald to the Wall I could pass from tree to tree without once touching ground: so vast is the great greenwood of England."

Jo looked at him in wonder; then followed his gaze to the convoy on the road.

"Still not past," said one of the outlaws. "How many have they killed? It's madness."

"Yes," said Robin, solemnly. "It is."

* * *

An hour later, with a horn of moon kindly lighting their path, the company from the forest had slipped from doorway to doorway through the town and were now among the snow-cloaked tombs and gravestones that clustered round a second church: this one at the street's west end, only a bowshot from the mighty barbican that guarded the castle gate.

"Why *this* way, Robin?" said one, very tense. "We'll never get through the gate, dark or light."

"I haven't the slightest idea," Robin replied. "I'm assuming the boy here is going to tell us: I assume that's why he's been sent."

"Sent?" said the outlaw.

"Yes." And Robin, turning to Jo and studying his face, said: "He's not of our world, are you, boy? He seems lost and bewildered by everything, but he knows more than he's telling. So come, boy: what's to be done?"

Jo was wide-eyed and open-mouthed. Not because he'd been put on the spot, not because he felt foolish and inadequate. In fact it was quite the opposite. It was because he did indeed know what to do.

Suddenly, inexplicably, he felt he could make a difference - could intervene as the note on the bike and the woman in the grotto had begged him to: he could, he felt, *be* more than Jo, and *do* more than anybody there.

8. Merlin

As Jo crumped his way through the firmest snow and drew near to the barbican, a figure in the shadows behind the portcullis was swinging a pale lantern. Jo supposed it was the gatekeeper, and stopped in his tracks. He wanted to glance back towards the churchyard for reassurance, but Robin and his men, crouched low behind the wall and gravestones, had urged him to give no hint of their presence. The plan, suggested to his own surprise by Jo, was naïvely simple - and not simple at all: he was to gain entry to the castle, and then find a way to let them in to rescue the Maid. That was as far as it went.

"Come closer, boy."

The gatekeeper's guttural tones sounded at least half friendly, so Jo slopped through the churned slush left by the company of hunters and stopped again a few yards from the gate.

"No, closer."

Not so friendly now. The gatekeeper's bulbous, lumpy face was pressed to one of the squares in the portcullis.

"I said, closer."

Jo took another step or two, then another. The gatekeeper raised his lantern, lighting his own bloated nose well enough but shedding only the merest glimmer on Jo.

"In days to come," said Jo, "when men step within range of an important door, lights will beam down instantly, and their presence

92

will be recorded by eye-machines."

The gatekeeper looked at him as if he were an idiot. "Are you a foreigner? What d'you want?"

"To come in," said Jo.

"No-one enters the castle after dark. Ever."

"But I'm - "

"Ever, I said!" And a gobbet of spittle flew through the portcullis and trickled down Jo's chest. There was a short burst of laughter from behind the gatekeeper, who was smirking with satisfaction, and two men-at-arms, helmeted and clad in mail and carrying long halberds, appeared at his shoulders. Something told Jo to ignore the grey trickle, and he spoke out boldly.

"King John won't thank you for refusing me entry. I have news that concerns him: important news."

"Don't tell me - it's going to snow tomorrow!"

Again a snort of laughter from the guards, and the gatekeeper roared approval of his own joke.

"I do have a forecast," said Jo calmly, "but not of the weather. I tell you, he'll want to hear it."

"And *I* tell *you*, take yourself off."

Words, Jo saw, were useless here. He plunged his hand into his pocket and pulled out the first thing he found: the pencil torch he'd taken for his shift on watch at the dig. He clicked it on and shone its blinding line of light straight in the gatekeeper's eyes. There was a babble of dismay.

"What's that? Hey! What're you doing?"

And as the gatekeeper reeled back, beating the beam from his eyes as if it were a hornet, Jo kept it trained full in his face, sharp, precise, until he blundered into a wall and dropped his lantern. It hissed briefly in the snow and went out. The guards muttered angrily, and Jo switched off his torch. To them he was silhouetted against the moonlit snow, but everything behind the portcullis was dark.

"What's going on?" said one. "What was that light?"

"It comes," said Jo, "and goes, when I choose." And he clicked it on again, making the tight, narrow beam dance across the vault of the archway. They turned and watched its weaving path. Then one of them, gauntleted hand shielding his eye, looked back at Jo and said:

"It's coming from his finger!"

Jo switched it off.

"What?" said the other.

"From his finger's end. It followed where he pointed!"

"Show us again, boy!"

"For what reward?" said Jo.

"Uh?"

"Will you let me in?"

"Look, we - "

On came the light again, Jo drawing huge figures of eight and writing his name in the air like a child with a sparkler, and as he did so he called out: "I predict, and I make light, and King John will wish to see me!"

Jo had never acted in his life, and couldn't understand where this theatricality was coming from - but he was grateful that it was; and the effect was immediate: the guards muttered something to the gatekeeper, and moments later came a clattering, winching rumble as the portcullis started to rise.

Across the snow and slush of the bailey they escorted him, through an intense smell of horse that told Jo they were passing stables; past buildings with chimneys belching smoke where great companies of men were carousing, rowdy; under the snowy branches of a massive oak that stood like a solitary hostage from the forest, inexplicably unfelled and unburnt; and on towards what he instantly recognised as the mound: the mound that was the site of his father's dig, that had a grotto at its base and a cistern at its head; but now there was no dig, no grotto and no cistern: it was the castle's motte, capped by a mighty stone keep, with a precipitous flight of wooden steps leading to the top. They made the thigh-straining climb; then words were exchanged with the guards at the keep's great door, and strange glances thrown; then Jo was ushered in.

They led him up an inner flight, his thighs and calves beginning to groan, and into a chamber where a figure sat with his back to an immense stone fireplace in which huge logs - sections of whole boughs, it seemed - were blazing, the flames surging deep into the colossal chimney.

"Why am I disturbed?" said the man, who was eating alone, his face uncouthly low over a platter of meat.

One of the guards stepped forward and began to murmur in the man's ear. Their eyes became fixed on Jo. The man wiped his fingers on the edge of the tablecloth and slowly cleared his throat. Then he took a long draught of what Jo assumed to be wine, put down the silver cup and sat staring at him. He was evidently considering his first move with extraordinary care. As it transpired, the question he finally asked could not have been more simple.

"Who *are* you?"

"Am I speaking to the king?" said Jo. One guard gasped, another laughed. The man at the table sat up straight.

"As opposed to whom?" he said with a dry smile.

"I don't know the present as well as the future - and some of the past," said Jo, who wondered where his words were coming from. "If you are the king, I have important news for you."

"If you know the future, you'll know what my answer's to be!" said the man, and looked to his guards for approval of his wit. They obliged.

"You are King John," said Jo, and praying that his scanty knowledge - largely the scraps that Annie had told him - was sound, he opened his mouth and let out a prophetic torrent. "And you will have a son called Henry, but not by the woman you married in the chapel here. You will meet a great host of barons at Runnymede in the year of our lord one thousand two hundred and fifteen and sign a great charter which will later acquire the utmost fame."

Jo stopped abruptly at this, as he realised he knew nothing more at all about King John. But he hadn't been contradicted yet, and had the king's rapt attention; so he ploughed on as the words took him.

"I will not tell you of your death, which God does not wish any man to know before his time." And, he thought, because I haven't got a clue how you died. "But this castle you have built will not last. Not a single stone of this keep will remain. The day will come when this mound will be covered in weeds and trees, and nothing will sit on its top but a cistern."

He was aware that, even by the standards of most prophecy, this sounded pretty eccentric, and he saw the king and his men exchange surprised glances. To his horror, the king asked him a question.

"Who will destroy it?"

Jo's mind went blank in a moment of abject panic; then inspiration struck:

"A great civil war will engulf this land, when the king will fight with his parliament - "

"His *parliament*?" The king appeared not to know the word.

"The great council," said Jo, wondering exactly how to define it, "who govern with him and agree to give him taxes - "

The king looked utterly appalled.

" - and parliament's armies will destroy this castle and many others, their cannons blasting great holes in - "

"*Cannons*?" said the king.

Jo stopped. Of course. He was on to a winner. But could he remember the details? Why oh why had they spent so much time in History doing the First World War and Nazi Germany?

"An amazing invention, my lord," he said, and started waving his arms in theatrical gestures. "Great tubes of iron will propel balls vast distances by the power of an exploding powder invented in China."

The king looked at Jo as if he were speaking in tongues.

"China?"

"Yes," said Jo, and rummaging deep in vague memory he translated it into the medieval: "Cathay."

"Cathay?"

Jo was surprised by this blank reaction. Just how late was the journey of -

"Marco Polo," he ventured, nervously, "a merchant from Venice," - and God, yes, thought Jo, it *was* Venice, how on earth did I remember that, and when did I ever read it? - "will discover a vast land in the East and return with the powder, and with coal." At least, he thought, I *think* all this is right.

The king looked thunderstruck. He shook his dark-locked head, not in disagreement, but as if trying to make sense of it all; then he turned to his guard and whispered for several moments. When he looked back at Jo, he nodded; but there was no smile to suggest pleasure at being convinced of Jo's powers: he seemed distinctly uneasy. And then Jo understood why, because, very dark and very low, he slowly said:

"When will I fight with this parliament?"

"Oh!" said Jo. "No, no, it won't be you! It will be a king of the house of Stuart, in the year of our lord one thousand six hundred and - " He paused for a split second and then it came: " - forty two."

The king's face suddenly lightened. He laughed a single, booming laugh of relief, passed his jewelled hand through his elegant beard, threw back his chair and strode stoutly round the table. He was about to clap Jo on the shoulders, but drew his hands back as if in some awe.

"So, then," he said after a puzzled moment, "if that is not your news, what have you to tell me?"

Jo hadn't the foggiest idea.

Then it came to him: he must tell the simple truth.

"You're about to be attacked," he said.

The king froze. "By whom?"

"By outlaws," Jo replied.

King John and his men relaxed, and frowned and smirked. "And what have you to do with outlaws?"

"Nothing. But I have visions of what is to come, and I have seen a host of men from the woods preparing an assault."

"Ah!" said the king, turning away and returning to the fire. "The homeless scum who poach my deer." He spat into the blaze and there was a momentary hiss. "They can prepare all they like. Not even Robin Hood himself could take this place."

"He will," said Jo, "by treachery from within."

The king came back and stood directly in front of Jo. He stared straight at him, hostility and fearful respect mixed in his black-browed eyes. And, very quietly, he said again:

"Who *are* you?"

And for a reason that Jo couldn't fathom he answered:

"Some men call me Merlin."

The effect was instant and alarming. The king staggered back as though Jo had hit him.

"Not possible!" he yelled. "You're dead and buried beneath this mound! Laurence! Laurence, I say!"

The king stood panting for several moments, the flames in the fireplace roaring behind his back, while his guards stood cowed and staring; then a side door opened and into the chamber stooped an old man dressed in deep royal blue from top to toe: a velvet hat covered a head which Jo guessed was bald beneath, and a long gown of silk and velvet swathed his bending frame.

"Laurence!" said the king. "This boy claims he's Merlin!"

Laurence stopped dead, and registered surprise but no alarm. "Does he so?"

"Is it possible?"

Laurence did not reply.

Tension mounted visibly in the king's face. "You've said yourself," and he stammered slightly, "that the stories are

98

impossibly confused. If he isn't buried beneath this mound he's been locked in stone by the temptress Nineve, never to be seen again in this world."

"Yes," Laurence slowly answered, and moved to the king's elbow, "though in the book that was brought to us at Candlemas, it said that Merlin retired to his *esplumoir*."

Now it was Jo's turn to be bewildered: this was becoming a foreign babble, and he had no idea why John was so alarmed about stories.

"And no-one," the king said, "was sure what that word meant."

"But its root is plain," said Laurence. "*Esplumer* concerns the shedding of feathers. It suggests to me the notion of moulting, of transformation and renewal."

"You mean," said the king, and Jo noticed that his hands were trembling, "Merlin is to be reborn?"

"In a sense," Laurence answered. "All the stories speak of transformation, of Merlin's power as a shape-changer."

At this, King John turned abruptly, and staring at Jo in alarm he whispered: "But why would he come?"

"What has he said?" Laurence asked, and he too was peering at Jo, studying him with fascination.

"That I'm about to be attacked by outlaws and betrayed! Is it because of Arthur? Is it for revenge?"

Jo couldn't keep up with this - until he suddenly recalled Annie's story on the mound: that there would have been a King Arthur had it not been for the wicked acts of John.

"The stories are not ciphers, my lord," Laurence said. "The Arthur of the Round Table is not the prince your nephew."

"Those stories *mean*," the king replied, his voice rising in agitation. "They have *meaning*. Arthur is sleeping, they say, waiting to rise again. And it seems that Merlin is already risen!"

He stormed across the chamber to the window, and peered out into the darkness as if looking for signs of the attack. Then he suddenly stopped, and turned back to Jo with deep suspicion. Something was not quite right.

"If you are who you say you are," he said, with slow cunning, "why have you given me warning?"

Jo again had no idea; it was a good question, and he waited, praying for inspiration. Again, the words came:

"It doesn't matter whether I warn you or not. What will happen will happen. I was here, so I told you."

"But to forewarn is to forearm!" said the king.

Damn it, this was true. What to say next?

"I merely said," Jo replied, hoping that an idea would come before he finished the next sentence or two, "that you were going to be attacked. It would have happened whether I'd told you or not. As for forearming, there's no need. Because I could also tell you, and with certainty - ", and as these words came, and the rest of the sentence emerged in his mind, Jo was staggered by the solution he had found, " - that you could leave every gate in the castle open and it would make no difference."

The king stood staring, brow furrowed and fingers pressing temples, trying to make sense of this. His chamberlain Laurence was more composed.

"My lord," he said, "how can we be sure that this is - "

"Merlin?" interrupted the king. "You didn't hear his prophecies: who else could know what he knows? He knows this castle's entire future. Tell me more, boy."

What more was there to tell? Again, Jo decided, the simple truth as he knew it.

"In the year of our lord one thousand seven hundred and thirty five, when this castle is long gone, a lady will make use of a spiral pathway to take walkers to the top of the mound; that will be in the days before the great cistern; and she will make a grotto of sea shells at the mound's foot; and the time will come, around the start of the third millennium, when people will park wheelybins by the bikesheds; and computers will be given a smart new home where your moat is dug; and scholars from Bristol and Oxford will come to dig into the mound, and will find antler picks but nothing more, but will send a mobile camera down a long tunnel to probe its lowest depths, to the consternation of Dag and Gareth and Mort with their motorbike and sidecar."

Laurence was dumbfounded. "Is he from the Tower of Babel? I understand nothing of this."

"What *I* understand," said the king, "is that he can see the future laid out before him, and he knows we're to be attacked. Will it be tonight?"

Jo nodded.

"And I'm to be betrayed?"

Jo nodded again.

"And it would make no difference if I left the gates wide open?"

He nodded a third time.

"We'll do so. Guards - "

"My lord - !" Laurence began to protest.

"We'll do so," the king repeated.

"You're endangering your life!"

"Not at all," said the king. "He's already told me that I'll still be alive in 1215, to sign a great document at... "

"Runnymede," said Jo as the king forgot.

" - Runnymede."

"Magna Carta," Jo added, enjoying the authority that Latin gave.

"This is madness!" Laurence cried. "You're - "

"Ah!" The king cut in, evidently amused by a sudden thought; and turning to Laurence with a ghastly smile he said: "But he's not told me of *your* future - such as it is at your age! What will become of Laurence, boy?"

Jo went blank. How could he possibly know? Then for no reason, and certainly with no malice, he suddenly said:

"You'll kill him."

A guard almost choked; then there was silence, while Laurence and the king stood staring at each other.

* * *

"Open the gate."

The command was simple enough, but the gatekeeper gawped at the king. There in the slush stood John in domestic gown and shoes, with no evident intention of venturing into the moonlit town, and no-one waiting to be admitted.

"And leave it open," he said. "Come on - do as I say."

So the gateman, for the second time that night, winched up the portcullis. Jo stood beside the king, looking out towards the churchyard where he supposed the outlaws would still be hiding. Behind them came sounds of carousing still, and Laurence, gathering breath after the brisk and freezing walk, said:

"Shouldn't we at least tell the men to prepare?"

"As you like - I leave it to you." And with that the king was gone, striding back through the hoof-churned snow into the bailey. A moment later Laurence turned on Jo, a savage rage in his watery eyes.

"I don't know who you are, boy, but all this talk of prophecy... Did you know of the king's credulity? Every time a troubadour comes with Arthur stories he imagines some deeper meaning! And you come claiming to be..." He stopped for a moment: he couldn't bring himself to utter the great enchanter's name. Then he continued, angrier still: "... and he swallows every notion! When an idea is sown in someone's head... People *make* predictions happen! Don't they? Don't they!"

Jo said nothing, and Laurence stood staring through his misting breath, impotent and uncertain; then he made an awkward shuffle sideways and said quietly, as if embarrassed to be asking: "*How* will he kill me?"

Jo knew nothing of this blue-clad, ageing man; he had no

reason to dislike him, to feel anything but pity for his obvious fear. For a moment Jo wanted to tell him it was all a big *ad lib*; but suddenly, out of the corner of his eye, he saw a movement near the churchyard. The outlaws. He took Laurence by the elbow and led him away from the gate.

"I didn't say it would be *tonight*," he said.

Laurence stopped and turned and almost smiled.

"As for your instinct to alert the men, it's wrong," said Jo. "If you do, there'll be unnecessary bloodshed. Let them eat and drink on, and all can happen peacefully."

Over Laurence's shoulder he could see two, three, four dark figures slip into the shadows of the archway. Then a whole, short scene was played out, entirely missed by Laurence: the gatekeeper appeared with his lantern and was smothered in an instant; his body was thrown back through the guardroom door; and the whole band of outlaws breezed like spirits into the courtyard, dispersed in all directions. Even Jo, watching, had no idea where they'd gone. But he felt elated, and proud: he had somehow manipulated matters to ensure Maid Marian's bloodless rescue.

But then, alarm.

If *they* were unaware of spirits, the animals weren't. From the stables came a frantic whinnying, and further off a single bark spread in seconds to infect a whole pack with demented howling. From the buildings around the bailey stumbled gaggles of men as yet not too far gone in meat and drink; some ran to the stables, others to see what had upset the dogs. But they could find nothing amiss, and the noise pounded on and brought more men staggering, cursing, into the bailey; then the company of guards on duty appeared along the walls, and angry accusations were hurled in all directions.

"Sort them out, you idle - !"

"Where the devil are the grooms?"

The howling now was deafening; and suddenly from the stables burst a dozen riderless horses, rearing and kicking in a frenzy. They careered into the crowd of men, lashing out as if possessed. Two or three men were down, wailing and moaning in the snow, the others scattering for shelter.

Laurence stood incredulous, and in a whimper, audible only to Jo at his side, he said: "For God's sake, stop this!"

But then, a mighty voice. The king was roaring:

"Shut the gates!"

Suddenly John was armed and mounted: it was one thing to have his castle attacked, but his horses and dogs were another matter.

"Shut the gates!" he yelled again. "D'you hear?"

Guards went clattering to the barbican; the men in the yard stopped yelling; the horses, amazingly, were calmed by the controlled example of the king's mount; the dogs' baying abated. But the strangest thing to Jo was the familiarity of the king's appearance: his great black horse, the dark iron armour... Jo knew he had seen them before.

But there was no time to recollect, for the king was riding straight towards him.

"What's this?" he said as he reined in before him, and he was snarling, furious and fearful. "Is it sorcery? Is the attack on my castle your doing alone?"

Jo was lost for words again - and this time none came.

"Speak!" hissed the king. "Merlin, speak!"

Jo's eyes darted around the darkness: had the outlaws truly vanished? If they could see and hear what was happening, why didn't they intervene and help him as he had helped them?

"What shall we do with him, Laurence?" snapped the king, as his horse stamped and snorted.

"If he is Merlin," Laurence replied, "bars and doors won't contain him."

"What, then?"

Laurence looked at Jo with sudden triumph and, seizing the opportunity, said:

"He needs to be destroyed."

Jo stepped back with a gasp.

"And without delay."

"Here!" yelled the king to the men in the shadows. "Seize this boy!"

And before Jo had time to speak or think he was taken in a violent hold, his arms locked hard behind his back, his neck twisted on to his shoulder. He was choking, barely able to breathe.

"Stand him against that tree," said the king, pointing to the solitary oak, "and fetch a dozen bows."

Jo gagged and gasped, his eyes streaming water. They were marching him across the bailey, thrusting him back with a bruising shove against the tree's great trunk, lashing ropes about him: in moments he was pinioned. And a group of men were walking forward with arrows nocked on their bowstrings, and the king was calling:

"Make ready!"

And they stood in line and took aim.

"No!" Jo could barely speak for disbelief; his voice hardly travelled beyond his clouding breath. "You can't do this!"

"All twelve arrows must hit his chest. Make no mistake. Stretch and loose in your own time."

And Jo gaped in churning panic as the strings drew back, the forearms tensed, and:

"If you shoot, the king will die."

The voice came from right beside him. And emanating from the very bark, it seemed, taking shape from the living wood itself, was Robin. His own bow was drawn, its arrow aimed directly at King John. The king's horse shied, snorting; and the king - and Laurence standing at his stirrup - looked stupefied. The archers' bows began to lower, and their eyes were no longer fixed on Jo, nor were they fixed on the king or Robin: they were staring over Jo's head into the branches of the oak; and Jo, screwing his head round and peering upwards, saw the snow-covered boughs lined with outlaws, arrows aiming down into their midst.

"Now," said Robin, very calmly, "tell us what you've done with her. Where is Maid Marian?"

"Ah!" said the king, controlling his horse and smiling sardonically. "So you've come to rescue her!"

"Nothing else would bring us to this monstrous place."

"I'm sorry to disappoint you," John sighed, "but she's out of reach. She's nowhere you can possibly go."

Jo had heard of an *oubliette*, a hole in a dungeon floor where a prisoner especially despised would be thrown and forgotten, never to be found. Surely the king wouldn't treat a woman so? But Robin had a different vision.

"You mean - you've killed her?" he said, anguish barely contained.

"Time would have done it if I had not."

"No!" roared Robin. "She would have lived forever except by human malice or neglect!"

"What a quaint idea," said the king, and he laughed softly. "But calm yourself. She's somewhere in that tower." He pointed towards the newest, most smooth-stoned, daunting part of his defences. "I'll leave it to you to guess where."

Robin gestured to his men in the tree, and they understood at once. Half of them stayed where they were, arrows trained on the throng in the yard; and half jumped down with the ease of birds and ran lightly across the snow towards the tower.

Robin untied Jo, then turned to John and said. "Dismount and come with me."

"It's rather novel, being given orders," said the king, swinging from the saddle and climbing down. "Not unpleasant, really, having one's life organised."

"You can come, too, boy," Robin said to Jo. "Prepare to see a wonder: we'll find her, have no fear."

But Jo sensed that the fear was Robin's.

They made their way to the tower. The outlaws had already

gone from chamber to chamber, landing to landing, up and down the spiral stairway.

"Nothing," they said. "No sign. No sound when we call."

Robin turned to John in a fury. "Where is she?"

"I'll give you a clue," he answered suavely. "Down's the way."

Jo followed Robin as he pushed John down the torch-lit, corkscrew steps, further than he could believe the tower needed to go. And at the very foot there was just one door, of heavy timber, painted black, with a massive iron lock and keyhole. Robin pointlessly turned the handle, then rounded on John and demanded:

"Give me the key!"

"Oh dear me, no," the king said calmly, "you can't go in there."

"Give it to me!"

"But it contains my greatest treasure."

"Not yours - mine!" cried Robin.

"My dear man." John shook his head and sighed. "It really wouldn't interest you to see what lies in there. In fact I fear it might distress you."

Robin looked into the king's green eyes, trying to see if he meant what he feared. They told him nothing; they only mocked. Breathing fast but deep, he drew a long dagger from its sheath and thrust it at the king's neck. It hovered, shaking, right beneath his beard, an inch from his throat.

"I really don't understand you," said the king. "Why don't you believe me?"

"Open that door."

The king sighed again. "You're so excitable."

"Open it!" And Robin jabbed the blade into the king's neck. Jo gasped as blood seeped down. The king at last was shocked, and his eyes showed fear and anger. He scowled, then reached down and lifted the skirt of his mailcoat. From a purse hugged tight to his waist he produced a large iron key.

"Be my guest," he said sourly, and wiped the blood from his neck with the back of his gauntleted hand, while Robin snatched the key and rammed it in the lock. It turned with the merest rattle and he pushed open the door.

Jo peered in under Robin's arm. Beyond the door was pitch black. Neither of them could see a thing.

"Bring a torch."

Jo did as Robin said: he hurried back to the stairway, past the darkly armoured king, and took a torch from its bracket on the wall. He was unsure how to handle the guttering flame, but he turned and tottered back into the room.

The moment he entered they saw it.

Piled almost to the ceiling, filling most of the room, were chests upon chests, sacks upon sacks, of what spillage on the floor told them was gold, silver and copper coin.

"You see?" said the king from the doorway. "Didn't I say it would distress you? Taxes from your beloved people. I know you don't approve, but it's in a good cause: the best weapons cost money, armies aren't cheap, and I have my campaigns in France to think of."

Robin was yelling now: "Tell me where she is!"

Jo could almost hear Robin's heart pounding. But the next voice was not the king's. From high above, in the courtyard it seemed, came a cry of: "Attack! We're under attack!"

And a moment later came a colossal rumbling crash as though an entire wall had collapsed.

"What's happening up there?" said the king; and as if their business in the tower had never been an issue he was running up the spiral stairway, back into the courtyard, with Robin and Jo following behind.

They emerged into pandemonium. Huge stones were plummeting into the bailey, flung from catapults somewhere in the darkness beyond: one had demolished a section of wall, another had scored a direct hit on the stables, and horses were running amok. Then fire: blazing arrows were scorching through the air, and while some landed harmless to steam in the snow, others were hissing in the thatch of the outbuildings and devouring them fast, and one thudded into a soldier's chest and pinned him to the ground, a horrified, screaming torch.

For what seemed like a minute the king stood paralysed; then, just as he opened his mouth to take command, the bombardment stopped. And a moment later a trumpet blared in the dark beyond the walls, as if calling everyone to order. The burning man was dead and screaming no more; the frenzied horses had disappeared to the far side of the castle; the only sound now was the blazing of thatch. And from the distance a voice cried:

"King John! King John! We have come to recover the maiden! Let us take her from where you've buried her, or we will destroy your castle utterly!"

Jo knew the voice. He ran forward and peered through the breach in the wall; and there astride a charger, his armoured company glinting in the moonlight, was Gareth, with Mort to one side and Dagonet the Fool on a pony to the other. And as he looked again at the dark-armoured king, Jo suddenly understood. The king was the knight who had killed the maiden in the fountain, and vowed to bury her in the tower's foundations; and the maiden in the fountain, the Maiden, was Marian, the Maid Marian - whom Robin had come to rescue from where he'd supposed her imprisoned. Both parties - Gareth and Mort and the court from the wasteland, and Robin and his men from the snowbound woodland - were set upon freeing the same being from the great tower of stone. But Robin hadn't known that she was dead.

The king was looking at Robin with eyebrows raised, enquiring, wondering if he'd understood.

"You've - *buried* her?" Robin said, struggling to speak.

The king just smiled.

And Robin Hood threw back his head and wailed.

So did the siren. A fire engine was storming past, thundering down the forest road, and Jo's head reeled in disarray, startled by the sudden colours and commotion. He coughed in disgust at the stale air in the 'phone booth. A police car roared by next, and picnickers and dog-walkers stopped and gawped, and muttered their assumptions to each other. Then some started pointing, animated, were stirred to action, packing their baskets, turning to leave. Then Jo saw it, too: above the trees, not far away, a cloud of smoke was spreading - the forest was on fire. Suddenly a face appeared at the door of the 'phone booth, heaved it open, pulled him out.

"Jo!" cried Annie. "Thank God we've found you! Come on - we've got to get moving!"

9. The Barrow

"Travellers," Don announced, as he and Richie and two of the other student dig-assistants clambered and squeezed into the back of the car behind Annie and Jo. "There's a New Age encampment back there and a couple of their vans are ablaze."

Annie started the engine and they pulled away. "Anybody hurt?" she said.

"Doesn't look like it," Don answered, and took a swig from a big plastic beer bottle, slopping a bit on Richie. "There was no-one in sight 'cept the police and firemen."

Richie had no doubts. "I 'spect they left some old stove going or something, forgot all about it. Useless peasants."

"No," said Don. "Apparently it was deliberate."

"What, vandals?"

"Who knows? I just heard the police saying."

"Good stuff!" said Richie. "Get rid o' the scum. Those travellers are nutters, half o' them, let out o' the loony bins and nowhere to go - 'cept Stonehenge at midsummer to prance about."

"I think they've gone down to the mound." It was Jo who said this. They all looked at him.

"You what?"

"They've gone to the dig," he said. He was staring straight ahead through the windscreen as they drove down the steep hill that led out of the forest and back into Marlborough. "There are *two* parties. The travellers aren't the ones who attacked it first," he continued, "but they've gone to join them - though they don't realise it."

Jo seemed to be talking to himself, as if working something out in his own head.

They looked at each other, then back at him, and Annie said, half amused, half concerned: "Are you okay, Jo?"

"Mmm?" he said. "Oh. Oh, yeah."

"First time I've heard him talk," Richie muttered in the back. "Exciting stuff."

"Looks like they'd've been moved on anyway," said Don, munching into a sandwich left over from the picnic. "The police were saying the whole forest's being closed down."

"You what?" said Richie.

"Yeah. Apparently it's all being sealed off because of disease."

"*Disease*?" said Annie. "What're you on about?"

"So we got the game of footie in just in time. Hey, Jo," said Don, "did you find the ball?"

* * *

As soon as they drove on to the gravel below the dig they knew there was something wrong: a police car was there again, with Jo's dad in frantic conversation, pointing first in one direction, then in another.

"It's ridiculous!" they heard him say as Annie turned off the engine and they opened their doors. "We need round-the-clock protection! This was done in broad daylight!"

"We'll do what we can, sir," one policeman said.

"I've never known anything like this!" he went on. "And we're bringing in expensive hire equipment: we can't afford to have it vandalised."

"We understand, sir," said another officer, patiently. "There'll be a car back shortly: we'll be making a full report - we'll make sure the next shift know what's happened."

"What *has* happened?" Annie asked Jo's dad as the police put on their caps and left.

He mouthed a silent expletive before replying. "Just after you'd gone - I hope you had a good time, by the way - "

They looked at each other, uncertain how to take this.

" - all the crud in creation arrived. Travellers, unmistakably: you should have seen the state of them. Dogs, kids, the lot. They started pulling down the barriers, the lamps, turned all our equipment upside down, threw tools down the mound... Bedlam. And I swear to God I saw two guys with an old motorbike and sidecar over there by the science block, watching. Same ones as before, without a doubt."

There was a pause. Annie was looking at Jo.

Jo's dad noticed this and said: "What's the matter?"

Annie said nothing but: "Jo?"

Jo's head was down; he didn't want to speak.

"What is it?" said his dad.

"Well..." Annie hesitated, not wanting to cause trouble. But then she said: "How did you know, Jo?"

Jo tried to look innocent, and failed.

"How did he know what?" said his dad.

"He said on the way back," Annie replied, "that some travellers in the forest had come down to join the first lot, to attack the dig."

"What?" his dad said. "What're you talking about?"

"I was just guessing," said Jo.

"Did you see something up there? If you did we need to tell the police. What did *you* see, Annie?"

"Me, nothing," she said. "But Jo was on his own for a bit - I found him in a telephone box."

Jo's dad shook his head. "I'm not getting this. Who were you 'phoning for God's sake?"

Jo was about to lie, but decided to tell the simple truth.

"Mum," he said. "I was trying to 'phone Mum."

"What the hell for?"

"To talk to her."

"Why would she want to talk to you? God I've had enough of this." He thumped Jo on the shoulder. "Get back to the hotel! I'll be there in ten minutes and you're going to tell me exactly what's been going on!"

And with everyone watching, he grabbed Jo by the arm and marched him away. Jo was sure he could hear Richie laughing.

* * *

As Jo ducked in through the hotel door and along the narrow entrance hall, the manager at the reception desk looked up and smiled.

"A letter for you," he said, and held it out.

"Oh," said Jo indifferently. "Thanks."

He assumed it was something for his dad, and it was only when he was half way up the stairs that he flipped it over to look at the stamp and stopped dead.

It was to him. And it was his mother's writing.

He shoved his thumb under the flap and ripped it open in a second. A man in a suit coming down the stairs barged past and said:

"Excuse me. Not the best place to stand, is it?"

Jo didn't hear him. His eyes were racing down the page. So he was equally deaf to…

"Good God - the people they have staying here."

…as the suit disappeared into the bar. Jo's eyes were filling up. He could barely read through the refracting blur. He wiped his eyes with a fist and read it all over again. Then he gave a bark of pain and outrage, and raced up the stairs, two at a time, on to the landing and along the corridor, rummaging in his pocket for the key; and with hands shaking so violently that he could hardly find the lock he threw open the door and rushed to the chest of drawers. Where were they, the other letters? Had he hidden them, his dad, or thrown them away?

"Why won't you write, Jo?" That's what the letter said. *"I've written four times in the last month, twice to the hotel this week. Why won't you answer?"*

He dug through the socks and underpants...

"If anything I've written has upset you, I understand - "

...a couple of ties and some handkerchiefs...

" - but you've got to believe what I said about your father."

...but no letters. No papers of any kind. He yelled and thumped the top of the chest of drawers, making the stupid ornaments rattle. The wardrobe. What about the wardrobe? He hadn't got long - his dad had said ten minutes. He flung it open, shoved his own clothes to one end of the rail, and reached for his father's jackets. One breast pocket and two side ones yielded nothing but a comb and a business card. But the suit...the suit that he never wore... There was nothing in the pockets, right or left, but as Jo patted the chest he could feel a lump. A wallet? No! He thrust his hand inside and pulled out... an envelope... unopened... addressed to Jo, in his mother's hand... postmarked three days earlier. If his father had destroyed the rest, he hadn't got round to this one yet. For a moment Jo lost his nerve: he dreaded looking inside. Then slowly, shaking, he slid a finger under the gum and opened the envelope. He held the paper between finger and thumb and pulled it out. And unfolded it. And read.

"My darling Jo, I'm sorry if - "

A key in the lock. His dad was back. Jo shut the wardrobe door and whipped the letter behind him. His dad came in. There was silence for a moment, then he tossed his hat on a bed and said with a groan:

"What a day."

He unbuttoned his shirt without a second's pause and then,

subdued, said:

"I've got to have a shower before we eat. And I need a drink."

"I could do with one myself," said Jo.

"What's stopping you? If you want to go down to the bar and wait - get yourself a Coke or whatever - they'll put it on the bill...but are you decent? Have you washed?"

"Yeah. Yeah, I'm okay."

His dad didn't turn to check. He was already in the bathroom. "I'll see you when I'm done," he called. "I won't be long."

Jo slipped the letter inside his shirt and was gone.

* * *

Jo's dad stood in the shower, shoulders hunched, and sighed as the warm water poured down his back, his buttocks and legs. He shuffled forward and let it drench his hair; then he turned round and, eyes lightly shut, let it blast the day's sweat from his face.

"Power shower," he murmured through dripping, barely open lips. He relished the words. "Power shower."

But as he reached for the soap in the ceramic dish built into the tiles, he flinched at a deep ache in his shoulder.

"Ah, *damn* it."

He angled his back so that the spray could work at the knotted muscle between spine and shoulder-blade, but it made no difference. And when the soap skipped from his hand to clatter on the shower floor, his knee groaned as he stooped. He flexed it once, and twice, and frowned at the weird sensation of the tender, fluid-filled joint. Everything hurt. Bits of his body were wearing out.

And then he caught sight of his reflection in the glazed shower-screen. Like a photograph in negative, this faint, dark image exaggerated features. It showed a deep line scarring one cheek, crow's feet stamped beside both eyes and bags beneath them; and his hair, matted by the power shower, clung in stripes to his pate and forehead, leaving broad, white bands of balding scalp.

He swore, and tried to spread and rearrange it, and stretched and massaged the wrinkled skin. It made no difference.

"God."

And as he stared at this shadowy self, he saw in it another, younger man, with loose-necked shirt and well-groomed hair, posing with the book that had made his name - *Neolithic Burials*; and another, younger still, with rugby shirt and nascent beard, who could have picked and chosen from any number of women and had opted for Jo's mum. Then back came the man with the clawing lines, the thinning hair, the baldness. And as the shower poured rain down the dark glass, the image blurred into another man entirely: now his mind saw his enemy, his rival, that young and photogenic don, that celebrity archaeologist whose face was in every supplement, his latest TV series nightly trailed, the accompanying book displayed in every window with its brilliant jacket of dawn-lit megaliths.

"Shaah!"

He slid the shower-screen back, and water sprayed across the floor. He cursed, and fumbled for the knob and turned it off. He stepped out and reached for a towel. The bar of soap was still in his hand, pink and slimy.

"Oh for God's sake."

He'd forgotten to wash, either body or hair. He dumped the soap on the side of the basin and stared into the bathroom mirror. It was opaque with steam. He squeaked it clear, then slouched forward, hands on the basin, and looked at himself. There were things the negative in the shower-screen hadn't shown: a broken blood vessel in one eye; patches of discoloured skin. But why, he thought, was he surprised? He was - what? - two-thirds of the way through life; and if his father's fate was an indicator, a damned sight more than that. In fact -

"Dear God."

- he was only nine years younger than his father had been when he'd...

He looked down at the sink. The tap was dripping. He turned it off, and as he watched the trickling dribble disappear, the memory came of his father wasting in a bed at home. It was summer, and sun was streaming on to the bedroom floor. His father wouldn't loose his hand. He had clutched his wrist; and his eyes, almost afraid to blink, were begging him not to go; and at the last, when he had tried to mouth some final words, it was clear that he was petrified, and staring into a void.

* * *

Downstairs in the bar Jo got a Coke, and sat himself in the corner facing the door, so he'd know when his dad was coming. Then he unfolded the letter and read.

Then he read it again. And again.

After several minutes Jo's Coke was still untouched, the ice had melted, and he was sitting just staring at the wall.

"I'm sorry if you don't believe me, and if you want to take your father's side I can't stop you. Maybe you felt the same as him, though I can't believe you'd have **done** *what he did..."*

Neither could Jo. He opened the letter on his lap and read it a fourth time.

"As soon as the scan showed the baby was going to be a girl he seemed to go cold, as if he'd no interest. I know it sounds crazy but it's true..."

Jo swallowed hard and read on.

"...And then when Kate turned out to be handicapped it was the end. He wouldn't accept that he could be responsible, that she was part of him. He wouldn't touch her, wouldn't look at her. I remember her crying, reaching out to him, and he would just turn away."

"God, that's better."

At the sound of the voice Jo slapped the letter shut and slid it under his thigh. His dad was walking up in a crisp new shirt and clean trousers.

"Now all I need's a decent drink and then I can wind down."

And he walked over to get himself a beer.

But others in the bar were *not* wound down: as Jo stashed the letter in his pocket and his father stood waiting for his pint to be pulled there was anxious, fevered talk about *disease*; about animals, abattoirs, transport, the ministry; and as his dad returned sucking the head from his beer, behind him there was an extraordinary, un-English scene as a trilby-hatted, tweed-jacketed, middle-aged man with a craggy face pushed a young bloke in a suit full in the chest, sending him staggering against the bar and spilling his drink.

"What the hell are you - !"

"You don't get it, do you?" The trilby-hatted man was fuming. "It'll be *your* livelihood down the pan as well! You can forget the flash suits!"

Jo's dad turned to watch, and chuckled to himself, seeming to enjoy it. Then he turned back and looked at Jo and, quite unexpectedly, he smiled. And he said softly:

"Jo."

"Yeah?"

"I'm sorry, son."

Jo blinked. "What?"

"I'm sorry - that I had a go at you."

Jo looked at him for a split second but couldn't hold his gaze. He looked away and cleared his throat. " 'S okay."

His dad took a drink; then: "Jo?"

"Mmm?"

"How old do I look?"

Jo frowned. He didn't understand the question. "Dunno."

"I mean - "

"I don't know how old you are - you're my dad."

"It's just..." His father was looking in his drink, embarrassed. "I feel sort of older suddenly."

"Working too hard," said Jo flatly, wanting the conversation to stop.

His father took a swig, and glanced out of the window. And then, with sudden intensity, he turned back and: "You've got to achieve what you want in life," he said. "And you've got to achieve it fast. Time doesn't bloody wait for you. And everything's there to distract you from what you know you really want."

Jo shook his head. "What're you talking about, Dad?"

"My dad never did a bloody thing. He was offered a place on an Arctic expedition and gave it up to get married."

He gave a sour laugh; but Jo's laugh was different, and his face was set and strong. He said: "What's so great about a trek across the ice floes?"

"Oh, come on!" his father answered. "She wouldn't let him go!"

"I always thought Gran had her head screwed on."

"You'd do that, would you?" his father glared. "Stay at home with the little woman?"

"What're you - ?"

"She crippled him," Jo's father said. "She crippled him. Pinned him down all through his life."

"Gran was great."

Jo's dad worked to contain his anger. "Do you mean that? Or are you just saying it to wind me up?"

Jo just shrugged.

His dad took a drink, but wouldn't let Jo off the hook. "Well?" he said. "What are you going to do with your life?"

Jo shrugged again. "Why do I have to do anything with it?"

"What?" said his father with distaste. "Haven't you got any ambition?"

Jo said simply: "No."

"Footballer, I suppose?" his father insisted, refusing to let it drop. "Delicate primadonna. Or are you honest enough to know you're not good enough?"

It wasn't just the question that Jo treated with contempt. He looked straight at his father while he took a long drink of Coke. His father registered the look and established his control with:

"What can I get you to eat, Jo?"

Jo understood the ploy and said, bluntly: "Whatever's going."

"Jesus, Jo!" His father snapped now. "You could take an interest in *something*, even if it's only the food!"

"Okay, okay," said Jo, all innocence. "Don't get stressed."

"Stressed? I wasn't until I sat down with you." Another swig. "But I'm entitled to be: I've got every mother's son and his mother trying to wreck the dig, and you a sulking millstone round my neck. If you don't want me to feed you go and look elsewhere - "

Jo was pushing back his chair.

" - but I shouldn't hope for too much from your mother: she's probably off on holiday with your sister and she's a lousy cook - "

Jo was opening the door.

" - and if you're not back by ten I'll murder you."

Round the back of the hotel he went, through a side gate into an unkempt garden, and collected his hired bike. One thing to be said about Wiltshire: the bike hadn't been nicked yet - in London it wouldn't have lasted ten minutes. He swung his leg over, scooted through the gate and up the alley, then kicked away up the High Street.

In two minutes he was there: beneath that looming mound. He stayed out of sight of Annie, Dave, Richie and the rest, all absorbed in arm-waving conversation with policemen near the tunnel's mouth, and pedalled quietly round to the far side. Then he stopped, and turned slowly in his saddle to peer out to the west and south like a Sioux warrior scanning the plains. What did he expect to see? Approaching knights? A band of outlaws? He wasn't expecting it, and he didn't see it. But he knew that Dag, Mort and Gareth were out there somewhere, and he wanted, desperately, to be with them. The dig, he knew now, had got to be stopped - and he sensed that it was up to him, even if he didn't quite know why.

But one thing he *did* see was a great plume of smoke: not smoke signals, that was for sure, but a wide pall of ominous blackness billowing up a couple of miles away. This wasn't the fire in the Savernake Forest - that was behind him, over to the east. This smoke was westward, and he instinctively felt it was sinister. He pushed away without another thought, and set off once more down the old Bath Road towards Silbury.

Nearer and nearer he came to the smoke-shroud, and soon he could see the flames that produced it. It was a huge fire - immense: a long, low pyre of burning matter stretched out in a deep, green field. And the smell was dreadful.

And then he was aware that it wasn't alone. A mile further on was another fire, and on a hill beyond that another, as if the country were being torched by a Viking horde.

And then he braked and had to stop. Crossing the road in front of him from one field to another came a tractor pulling a cartload of sheep: not standing and bleating in a woolly crowd but heaped in a bloated mound of fleece, legs sticking out, black against the matted white, chaotically, in all directions. They were dead. Jo stared as the cart went jolting, a lumbering tumbrel, over what had once been pasture and on towards the waiting fire.

As he drew near the next smoke, a mile further on, he could make out the shapes of creatures a good deal bigger than sheep. At the base of this pyre were cattle: great white Charolais, dappled Friesians, mighty bulls and fawn-like calves, all burning in a long and monstrous barrow.

The stench carried on the light, warm wind was more than Jo could bear, and he pedalled fast down one hill and up another to get himself beyond it; and as he crested a ridge crowned by barrows from an earlier age he could see Silbury Hill below him. He rested his aching thighs and free-wheeled down the next stretch, and then suddenly began to wonder if he'd be able to find Dag's caravan again. The sun was starting to sink, but light would make no difference: he'd only been there in the dark, and realised now that he didn't really know where the camp had been.

Silbury dipped out of sight behind a bend, then loomed into view once more. She was magnificent, silent, latently potent.

There were trees dotted here and there, a clump of sorts away to the right, and a scrubby copse ahead, but nothing reminded him of Dag's camping place.

"Darn it!" he muttered to himself. "Dag, where are you?"

Then something caught his eye to the left.

At the top of a ridge, outlined against the failing light, was a long, low mound. It seemed oddly dark and threatening. Was it another pile of cattle, waiting to be burnt? For some reason Jo felt drawn towards it: for all its dismal menace it was fascinating: as fascinating in its way as Silbury's great belly.

A footpath led in its direction, and Jo turned off the road and up to the gate at the path's foot. Then he stopped. A fresh, white paper sign with bright red lettering had been newly taped to the gatepost.

The footpath was closed. An outbreak of Foot and Mouth Disease.

The sign wasn't meant for cyclists, though, thought Jo. Humans couldn't catch foot and mouth - only animals: "Must be for dog-walkers," he muttered. Then he saw great bales of hay piled across the path. So maybe they didn't want bikes either. He parked it against a fence, clambered over the bales and carried on, across a narrow stream and then uphill.

The path grew surprisingly steep and narrow. It was well trodden, though, and as he drew nearer to the mound on the ridge-top he could see why: this was no cattle-pyre but another ancient earthwork monument - not round and full like its neighbour Silbury, but long, spindly, low, lying stretched along the ridge like a thin, dismembered corpse with a crooked spine.

As he drew closer an official display board gave its name: the West Kennet Long Barrow.

"Not the zappiest title in the world," Jo muttered to himself.

It also gave its function: a Stone Age burial chamber.

As night began to fall everything was acquiring a strange scale, and the four huge, oddly shaped slabs planted upright together at the barrow's mouth had the most impressive presence. In Jo's mind their outline suggested the back and head of an ancient, heavy-shouldered ox. Was it standing there on guard, minding the entrance? He stepped towards it, but then stopped. He was strangely in awe of this stone beast. He was aware, too, that his footfalls on the pebbly earth were the only sounds to be heard: all around him was a vast silence: no bleating or lowing anywhere: the countryside was dead.

He took a breath, and stepped on; he moved up to the ox's head and patted the furry lichen on its muzzle. Then suddenly he went cold. His back was to the barrow's entrance. He spun round. And then felt silly: it was silly, he thought, to be nervous. The long-dead bodies buried there would surely be in museums now, plundered by archaeologists years ago.

The barrow's mouth was very dark, a dank slit between fat stone lips. But it would be ridiculous not to look inside.

In a couple of paces he was there, bending his head to peer into the dark. A few feet further in, he could see a shaft of pale light falling on the floor, and as he stooped and crept into the barrow's passage he realised that someone in the past century had cut a skylight in the roof and filled it with a thick pane of glass. Just enough of the day's last light seeped through to reveal the burial chamber's shape. The central passage had five alcoves leading off: one at the head, and two on each side like pairs of gently splayed limbs.

The moist darkness had never been warmed; yet for all its chill stillness Jo felt curiously calm. It was a safe, embracing place, and if it had once been filled with dead their ghosts were not offended by his presence. He seemed, in fact, quite welcome there; and as he crouched in its very middle he felt lulled and soothed, lulled and soothed into the sweetest, deepest drowsiness. Despite the cold, he curled himself on the hard earth floor; and before he knew it he was asleep, his knees hugged tight, his head on his chest, a floating foetus waiting to be born.

It was then the hag came in. Stooping through the barrow's mouth, the great stone ox now dark behind her, she shuffled her tall, lean frame along the passage. When she reached Jo's feet she stopped to look down at him, strands of her lifeless hair shrouding her face. Then she reached into the pouch that hung at her side, and from it she drew forth a snake, an adder, its tongue alert and flickering. She set it on the floor beside Jo's spine. Following the line of his curving back it slithered along the ground towards his neck. There it paused, disturbed, excited, flickering more; then it traced the outline of his dishevelled head and continued its circuit towards his heart and belly. For a moment it stopped again, poised to slide between his close-hugged arms and knees. Then it did. It burrowed between his sleeping limbs and made straight for his navel. Still he slept; still she watched. And in the shadows of Jo's foetal body the adder split. From behind its head its outgrown skin broke open, and from the near-transparent scales it emerged, new and greater, and slowly crested his pelvis before sliding back to earth. She bent down, gathered it gently into her old, old hands and let it slide back into her pouch. Then she passed her hand over Jo's brow... and in his sleeping mind he saw it all.

He could *be* anyone. He could *do* anything. He would indeed be Merlin, and he was needed now, at the castle.

She spoke to him in his dream, in a voice that was neither old nor young and not distinctly female, and gently admonished him.

"They are waiting for you, Merlin. Why do you delay? You must bring the treasure-tower down and release the Maiden's spirit. The outlaw has given way to despair - he will be of no use now; and the knights are no match for the castle's power - not without you. You alone are the one."

"Bloody hippy!" Angry hands were grabbing him and shaking him awake, then dragging him, cracking his knees on the barrow's stone mouth, out into the open air. "Christ, they start you young, dun't they?"

Jo grunted and gasped, bemused, as a flat-capped farmer hoiked him to his feet and shoved him away from the ox-slabs.

"Can't you damn well read? An't you got no sense at all? I thought I saw some idiot comin' up here. Signs bloody everywhere: keep off o' the land! We got the foot and mouth ruinin' us all and you bloody travellers dun't give a monkey's!"

He stopped for a moment, and saw Jo's blank gape.

"Whassup? I an't hurt you, surely?"

"No, no, I just...". Jo stood there, sagging, and gave a violent shudder. He was chilled to the bone.

"Christ, I an't surprised you're frozen. What the 'ell you doin' sleepin' in there? 'Spectin' some bloody revelation or whatnot?"

Jo swayed a bit.

"Oh my God, what're you on?" said the farmer. "You on somethin', are you?"

Jo's only reply was a shake of the head and a look like a lost eleven-year-old.

To his own surprise the farmer began to mellow. He sniffed and shuffled; then said: "You awright, son?"

Jo shook his head again.

"Where you frum?"

"Merlin," said Jo, then blinked at the word. Then he remembered. "Oh - yeah - the Merlin - the Merlin Hotel."

"Ah," said the farmer. "Marlborough."

"Mmm."

"Well then," he said, and sniffed again. "Well then." What was he to do? He wasn't used to being a Samaritan. Then: "Reckon I'd better take you 'ome." Then:

"I can't stay," murmured Jo. "I'm needed." And:

"Christ!" said the farmer: he suddenly had to catch Jo as he toppled forward and fell.

10. The Trap

And Jo was there. He was Merlin, standing in the snow, amazed and alarmed to find himself alone with King John beside the smashed castle wall. Robin and the outlaws were nowhere to be seen.

"They do move fast, I must say," said John, sardonic as ever. "They melted away as swiftly as they came. Well, that's despair for you. No moral fibre! Such a lot of upset over a girl!"

Then he turned to look through the breach in the wall.

"Impressive machinery they've got over there," he said. "Shame they couldn't make up the numbers."

He was right. Away in the moonlit snow beyond the moat Gareth and Mort, with Dagonet beside them, were backed by no great armoured host but by a small, if shining, company of little more than four score knights.

"No great cause for alarm, I feel," John breezed. He called across the courtyard. "Block the breach with waggons for the present. Put out the thatch-fires. Gather in the horses. And don't waste arrows by returning shot." Then he turned back to Jo and said, in a tone of quiet control: "And you, Merlin, will come with me."

Across the moon-bright bailey they strode, then up the steep steps to the keep, where in a moment Jo once more found himself standing before the blazing log-pile in the soaring fireplace, and face to face again with the age-bent, blue-clad Laurence.

"I should have had you killed," John said.

Jo turned and looked at him.

"But you interest me, very much. It seems to me," the king continued, as he sat down slowly with his back to the fire, "that if I'm still to be alive - and still the king - in 1215 as you prophesied, then I have nothing to fear from you. But tell me one thing: the Merlin of the stories I have heard saved the tower of King Vortigern from repeated collapse - he revealed a pair of dragons sleeping in an underground lake, disturbing the tower's foundations. Can you ensure that *my* tower never falls? My treasury must never be in danger."

Jo knew nothing of this story, but the answer came with an ease that astounded him.

"There are no dragons below *your* tower, my lord. But there is a maiden. And for as long as she lies buried there, the army that besieges you will be determined to cast it down. They may not be many, but their catapults and siege-machines are very strong - strong enough to accomplish what you fear."

Jo couldn't understand where the words were coming from.

"So what should I do?" said the king, sharp and edgy. "Have my forces counter-attack and raise the siege?"

"I cannot tell you what you *should* do: only what you *will* do."

For a moment the king frowned, perplexed. Then his mouth spread in a beaming smile at Merlin's promise of sure prediction. "Go on!"

And Jo continued: "You will lure them in by feigning your own death. Your forces will signal surrender. And once your enemy are inside the gates, your men will move in to slaughter them."

Jo was appalled by this plan. Why had he said such a dreadful thing? John wondered the same.

"Why should you tell me this?" he asked, leaning forward with slow suspicion. "Why should you give me this idea?"

"Because - because it's true," said Jo, trying to disguise his own alarm. "It's what will happen, whether I tell you or not. It's the future."

"And what will make them think me dead?"

Jo had, for a moment, no idea. Then his eye fell upon Laurence, whose death at John's hands he had earlier foretold, and he suddenly said:

"Treachery. Laurence will be seen to kill you."

Neither Laurence nor John knew what to make of this. The great seer's predictions were bewilderingly confused. Each stared at the other, as if to read his mind, then laughed with feigned derision, to conceal their dark and instant fears.

"And when is this, Merlin?" said John, turning back to Jo. "When is this to happen?"

"As soon as it is light enough to see."

The king glanced towards the window and rose abruptly from his chair, and he and Laurence raced each other, jostling on the stone window-seat as they leaned forward and peered out. The moon had vanished into dense cloud, and beyond the walls, beyond the moat, all was darkness.

"A little while yet," John said. "Time enough to sleep before I'm - " He paused, as if tasting the peculiar thought. " - Seen to die."

Old Laurence's behaviour then was strange. Without a word he shuffled across to the chamber door and opened it; then he turned, stared straight at John and went out backwards, bowing like a hammy actor, intoning in a hollow voice: "I'll go to bed, then, by your leave, my lord."

It was so ludicrous that John laughed; and as the door closed he said: "Anyone would think he didn't trust me - or," he added, "that I shouldn't trust him."

For a short while the king sat gazing into the fire, its dancing light warping his features. Jo didn't disturb him: he was too busy in his own mind, shuffling his mysterious predictions. Then the king rose sharply and strode from the room, saying nothing more than: "Wait here."

Moments later the chamber door swung open and two guards came in and stood, staring at Jo. Their faces were heavy with concern. Then they shut the door behind them. And stood.

"Come and sit by the fire," Jo said.

They started, and looked at each other in awe. Even the most trivial utterance by Merlin, Jo realised, assumed great weight. They crept to the royal fireside chairs and perched, tense and sheepish.

Jo wandered over to the window. Down below all was returning to order: the horses that had bolted from the burning stables had been gathered in and tethered to great stakes; the thatch-fires were doused and barely smoking; and all the royal forces were alert and sober, ranged around the walls and at the barricade erected at the breach. And the sun was beginning to rise above the forest. In the misty light Jo could see King John in urgent conversation with his captains. Merlin's plan, he guessed, was being set in place: surrender would in time be signalled, and Gareth, Mort, Dag and the rest of their shining company would be drawn into a trap.

What had made him say it?

Minutes later, John was back; and in his eyes was a look of perfect certainty, a stone determination. He looked at Merlin for the merest second, smiled through his short, neat beard, then beckoned to the guards, who started up immediately and followed him. They left the chamber door ajar, and Jo, filled with an all too accountable fear, counted to ten to let them get ahead, and then quietly slipped out after them.

The spiral stair was very dark. He had not climbed far before he heard whispers above him. Supporting himself on the central column he perched on the narrowest part of a step and twisted round to look up. It was impossible to see: the angle was too tight. He crept on just a few steps higher and found his nose an inch from a chain-mailed leg. The guards had stopped. King John was whispering to them, inaudibly. Jo didn't move. But the guards did: with the utmost stealth they mounted another step or two and then - what? Jo heard a slight metallic tap as if a door-latch were lifting, and the tiniest creak of a turning hinge.

Suddenly, Jo knew exactly what was happening - and he knew that it was his fault.

There was a great cry of fear and outrage, the terrifying glide of sword from sheath, then a howling shout, muffled in an instant. Jo couldn't help himself: he ran up the last steps and hovered in the doorway, to see John watching as the guards pinned Laurence to his bed, a fat white bolster stifling his face.

"Enough! We don't want him dead just yet!" said the king. The bolster was swung aside and Laurence lay, gasping for air, as one guard set a sword-point at his throat. "Now dress him as befits a king!"

"No!" cried Laurence in feeble protest.

"And meanwhile I'll just don your - " John paused, less than impressed as he looked closely at a worn collar, " - your *beautiful* blue gown - good God, man, is this the best you can afford on all I give you? - and see if I can adopt that very fetching stoop of yours."

"My lord," gabbled Laurence, "I've no intention of betraying you, ever, on my life - "

"Laurence my dear man, you clearly have, for why else would I kill you as Merlin has prophesied I shall?"

At this Jo ducked from the room and pressed himself into the tiny space behind the door frame. He was sweating from shock: shock at the consequences of his speech. It was uncanny: his two predictions - that John would kill Laurence but would be seen to be killed by him - had come randomly, as if from nowhere...and yet made perfect, terrible sense.

"His prophecies, indeed, are brilliant, are they not?" John smiled. "For your death is intimately bound up with his plan. You see that, surely?"

"My lord, I beg you - !"

"No," said the king with suave distaste. "No, please don't do that."

Jo peered round the doorpost into the room. Laurence's blue gown was now draped on the king's shoulders, and a velvet hat ensconced upon his head. And Laurence was being forcibly dressed in John's deep, rich cloak.

"From a distance," pondered the king, turning on one toe to display his new costume, "what would you say?"

The guards just nodded; one of them smiled.

"From the window, do you think," John asked them, "or from the roof? The roof would be more spectacular, of course."

Laurence gave a wordless cry.

"Yes," the king decided, "bring him to the roof."

Jo swung back behind the door frame. But it was no hiding-place. John didn't see him as he strode back to the spiral stair, but Laurence did - and he cursed him.

"This is your doing, Merlin!" he cried. "Damn your mother, and damn your demon father!"

"An interesting notion," John called back. "How can you damn a demon?"

The guards were less glib. They stared at Jo with their previous awe, and one growled low, in apparent fear: "Demon father, Hequibedes!" Jo gawped, uncomprehending. "Mother a virgin, father a demon," the guard went on, and seeing Jo's blank look he said: "Don't pretend it's not true! It's where you get your powers from - all the stories say it!"

They were winding their way up the stair - not the easiest route with an unwilling captive - and Jo followed them, the guard appearing more concerned with his presence than with the wrenching struggles of Laurence. Then the king pushed open a smooth-hinged door and pale dawn light slanted down into the spiral: they were on the roof.

"They won't believe you!" Laurence yelled at the king. "They won't be fooled!"

"Not if they hear your aged screaming, certainly," said the
king, and he stepped forward; and while the guards kept the old
man pinioned he pulled a glove from his hand and rammed it into
Laurence's mouth. "You've been a loyal chamberlain to me these
several years," he said, "and now's the time to do me the greatest
service."

Laurence was heaving, scarcely able to breathe. John nodded
to the guards, and they dragged the old man to the edge of the
keep's roof - a dizzying height, Jo realised, as he looked out miles
to the west and Silbury, and miles to the east and Savernake.

"Now we come to the tricky part!" said John perkily; and as if
it were some petty practical joke: "I've got the stoop: can I do the
voice?"

He looked over the crenellated rim and in a moment saw the
besiegers; they were beginning to deploy forces outside the
barbican - to stop anyone entering or leaving the castle - and were
heaving their catapults to face John's treasure-tower, preparing an
attempt to smash it down.

"Get ready," he suddenly said to the guards. "Remember the
parts you have to play."

Then he stood up tall in his chamberlain's blue gown and hat
and, taking an immense lungful of freezing dawn air, bellowed out
across the bailey, over the walls and beyond the moat: "Truce! A
truce! We beg a truce!"

Jo had always noted the curious way in which you knew that
someone was looking at you, even from a mile away, even if you
couldn't see their eyes - and he knew now that every eye in the
besieging army was fixed upon this roof.

"We have no wish," the costumed king roared on,
impressively conjuring an aged hoarseness, "to have this castle
ruined and needless bloodspill. Only one man need die - the tyrant
John!"

At this he gestured to the guards, and Laurence, the very

image of the king, was hoisted on to the battlements, grunting wildly through the glove in abject terror.

"The enemy of peace and justice!" John bawled. "The killer of his nephew Arthur! He shall be king no more: we cast him out - and down!"

For a terrible second Jo felt that Merlin should intervene, cast a spell, make a mystical utterance to stop it all. But it was too late: a moment was all it took for the guards to push John's chamberlain into air. From beyond the moat Gareth, Mort and Dagonet would have seen the body of the king plummet down the keep in a swirl of velvet, hit the mound beneath, and tumble down its snowy side to land out of sight in the surrounding ditch.

"You are welcome here: the gate is open!"

So cried the king; and as he signalled to a captain waiting in the bailey, all was set in motion: the shining company led by Gareth would be drawn into the trap.

But Jo was past caring. He wanted the whole mad business to be over. While John and the two guards returned to the spiral stair, Jo sank down on the roof, his back to the battlements, and put his head between his knees. He was shivering uncontrollably with shock - and he realised, too, how bitterly cold he was.

"I can't stop shaking," he said.

And his father said: "If you're expecting any sympathy... If it hadn't been for that farmer chap you'd have pneumonia."

What? What was going on? Jo struggled to focus: rose-pink walls... air freshener... bright electric light...

"Why should he have to do that, Jo? Why should he have to drive you home because you're too damn stupid to look after yourself...?"

...tea bags and tourist brochures planted on the dressing table...

"...I wouldn't mind so much but it makes *me* look an idiot: I'm supposed to be looking after you, to know where you are..."

... He was back in the hotel room, in the bed with the nylon coverlet...

"...I could tell by the way he looked at me he thought I was a loser. Get this down you."

Jo's dad handed him a mug of hot chocolate. Jo took it and looked at it blankly. Then he began to focus again. And it didn't look right.

"It's not properly dissolved," he noted. "It's all scummy on the top."

His dad looked incredulous. "Are you trying to wind me up?" he said.

"It's that instant stuff, isn't it? Made with hot water."

His father's eyes blazed: he was about to reply with something savage, but stopped and just shook his head.

"Get yourself under those covers," he said; and then, with a sudden softness, he murmured: "I don't want you getting ill." He blinked and looked away. "I hate it when you're ill." And he sat down gently on the edge of the bed. For a few moments he watched Jo sipping through the steam. Then he said: "I'll ask reception to bring up a hot water bottle." He gave a half-laugh. "Dear God," he muttered, "a hot water bottle in August."

"I don't need one."

"Yes you do - and a brain to go with it."

"Thanks, Dad."

"Look, if you think I'm unreasonable, just put yourself in my place for a second. I've got rather a lot on my plate, wouldn't you say? The dig's being fouled up - though we'll get it sorted; but it means I've got the police to deal with - a major operation they're mounting now, and about time too: just you wait till they get the scum who're behind it... But in the middle of it all I've got you disappearing at all hours and - "

"Yeah, yeah, all right, Dad - I get the point."

"But no apology, I take it? That would be too much to expect."

"An apology?" said Jo. "Am I the only one with something to be sorry for?"

"What are you on about?"

There was a silence. Jo blew through the steam and sucked at the hot chocolate.

"Well anyway," his father said, calming down again and putting on a jacket, "I've got to be off. Now just stay put, Jo, will you? If you're not here when I get back I'll - "

"Where are you going?"

"Well, there's a good chance I'm going to the dig, wouldn't you think? It's all set up."

"What is?" said Jo, with an edge of alarm.

"The police are hiding men all round the mound. We're going to leave all our stuff and make it look barely guarded, and when the morons whoever they are come looking for fun they'll have 'em. Criminal damage, breach of the peace, hopefully a bit of resisting arrest, doubtless no road tax on their vehicles, no insurance... That'll do nicely." He opened the door, and muttered to himself: "Criminal damage? That's what we ought to *inflict*."

He closed the door behind him. For a few moments Jo sat motionless in bed. Then he put down the hot chocolate and threw back the covers.

* * *

By the time Jo reached the College it was very dark. Knowing police were hidden but not knowing where - and knowing that if his father saw him he'd go berserk - made things difficult: he couldn't show himself openly near his dad, but if he acted at all suspiciously he might get stopped. What to do?

The first thing was to keep his distance. He crept along a mossy path that ran behind the College chapel. As he passed beneath its shadow he glanced up at its lofty bulk. The mighty Victorian place of worship soared like a liner, adorned with glass and gargoyles and radiant with certainties - and with accusations: Jo sensed it saw his furtive thoughts... but no – this was no time for knee-jerk guilt. He dodged swiftly past the big west doors and slipped into the darkness of its south porch. From there he could see across the rose garden that lay in what had once been moat, and over to the mound and the dig site.

It was strange. A couple of lamps were blazing at the tunnel's mouth, but there was no-one to be seen. Were they trying to attract them there like moths to a bulb? Did they think they'd be that stupid? Maybe they would be.

Just then a car passed behind him along the main Bath Road, then another, and another, and Jo realised he was on the wrong side of the mound. If he wanted to stop and warn Gareth and Mort as they approached, he'd need to be on the other side: there was no way they'd come along the road - they'd surely take the back way as they'd done the night they biked him home past the tennis courts and dropped him by the river.

But what about the travellers who had come down from the forest? Would they just go blundering in regardless?

Whatever was going to happen it wouldn't be in the chapel porch, that was certain - he was no use to anyone there; so he quietly padded down a craggy flight of broken steps and began a circular route across a playing field. A football pitch was freshly marked, ready for the coming season. The moon came out, as bright as floodlights, and as he jogged across the penalty box Jo jumped and headed an imaginary goal, powering the ball past the 'keeper's dive and into the bottom corner. 3-2 and a last-minute winner! Oh for a game of football and to be done with all of this. But he jogged on, round the back of a massive stack of leaves and grass - a year and a half of groundsmen's work - and made his way to the river and the bridge.

The noise grew louder and louder as he approached. By the time he reached it and stood, hands on hips, recovering breath, it was a churning, floundering roar. The water poured in a rushing rumble, foaming and flashing blue in the moonlight as it surged over a mini-weir. Jo's breath slowed and softened now and he sat on the bridge's parapet. It was wide enough to lie on, and he swung his legs round and stretched out with a sigh, and gazed through arching branches and away up to the moon. Beneath him the river roared on.

But soon Jo shifted, and sat up again: he wasn't comfortable. It wasn't the hardness of the rough stone wall: it was the noise. The roar was all-obliterating; he could hear nothing else. He glanced around. The trees along the banks were full of shadows, and every shadow assumed a shape. He spun to look in one direction, then another. Oh, but it was ridiculous, he told himself: what was there to fear? If Gareth and Mort and Dag appeared they'd be pleased to see him, not threatening.

He stood. He paced. He sat down on the wall again.

Minutes passed pointlessly, as he shuffled and shifted, waiting for people who might never come. And he felt cold again - really cold.

"God, I'm shaking."

He almost wanted to cry at his own stupidity - maybe his dad was right, that he'd got no sense at all; he should be back in bed with a hot water bo-...

He stood up and stayed stock still. He knew that something was watching him.

"Dag?" he called, softly. "Are you there?"

The river gushed below.

"Gareth? Mort? It's me, Jo - Joel."

The moon was suddenly engulfed in cloud, and the darkness was complete. The shadows were gone. There was only noise, shapeless and smothering.

"Dag?"

Then a footfall - not on earth or path but in water. And another. Amid the constant storming was a different sound, quite certainly: the plashing of someone wading in the river. He looked over the side of the bridge. No-one. Along the banks. No-one. He backed away, and as he turned to run back towards civilisation his knees went rigid and his mouth gaped wide. Blocking the end of the bridge was a man. His outline was different from any he had ever seen: tall but sturdy, hair long and loose, shoulders draped with a crumpled cloak but arms and legs quite bare. He was looking straight at Jo. In the darkness his face was invisible, but it wasn't Dag, it wasn't Gareth and it wasn't Mort. Then he moved. He was walking, dripping, straight towards Jo.

"I don't know you," said Jo. "Can you keep away, please?"

The man stopped. He drew his hand from behind his back. He was holding something. And suddenly Jo remembered he had a torch. He plunged his hand in his pocket, pulled it out and fumbled to switch it on. Then he swung the shaking beam to shine on... the woman. It was a woman. And she raised her hands and held up... the vessel he had seen before. As it met the torch-beam the reflection was dazzling, and Jo turned his head away with a gasp. Then he looked back; and she pointed - first to the torch and then toward the mound - and Jo in an instant understood. He was needed there, now, and he could imagine why. Without another word or another thought he ran past her and away.

He was sprinting, his feet pounding, his heart pumping, and he ran without any thought for the noise he made; and there, hidden behind machinery at the end of the flooded building site, was a motorbike and sidecar, and two men were crouching, hiding behind it - surely it was Gareth and Mort; but just as Jo was about to call, he realised one was talking into a radio; then the other turned, and Jo saw the outline of a cap: they were police. He stopped dead. And they saw him. One stood up, glancing around nervously.

"What do *you* want, son?" The voice was soft and secretive.

"Oh, er, nothing," Jo panted. "Just on my way home."

"Well make sure you are, then," the policeman whispered. "Late enough, isn't it?"

"Yeah, yeah, my mum'll go mad", he said, and ran off towards the wheelybins.

"Hey, not that way! That's a dead end, son," the policeman

hissed. "What're you up to?"

But Jo kept going, and as soon as he was out of sight he dodged behind a bin, stale and stinking. He heard gently jogging boots coming up, then slowing, stopping, and the crackling babble of a radio.

"No, it's okay," he heard a moment later. "It's just a kid. Don't know what he's up to, though... What? No - no travellers," the policeman whispered as he shuffled into the shadows. "I reckon we've seen the last o' that lot: they've got more to worry about right now than muckin' up a dig. Vans burnt out an' that, up in Savernake... Yeah, that's right. An' they've got to find somewhere to camp, what with all the foot an' mouth an' that: the whole countryside's closed down... Yeah. So the blokes with this famous sidecar are going to be on their own! You should see the state of it - museum job! ... No - no sign of 'em. But they must be close: they'd only just arrived when we found it: the engine was still warm."

"Hey! Rob!" It was a hushed call from the policeman's partner. Jo peered round the bin and saw the other officer pointing urgently to the right. "It's them!"

"It's them!" was whispered into the radio. "Brilliant! Right - remember: we let 'em get stuck in, but at the first sign of damage Willis is going to blow the whistle and we all go in together. They haven't got a prayer! Come on!"

And Jo saw them stalk away into the darkness. For a split second Jo's impulse was to run and yell, just run and yell a warning; but then he realised that even if he did, Dag and the others would never get away: if there were as many police as it seemed, they'd be caught before they could reach... the bike...

The *bike*! The motorsickle! That was it!

Jo scurried out from behind the bin and dashed back to the end of the building site. He stood there, panting, and looked at Mort's machine. Was he really going to do this? He'd never ridden a motorbike in his life. How could he even start it without a key?

Then he noticed something strange. Attached to the handlebar by a dangling string was a ring-pull from a drinks can. He guessed at once why it was there: how long would it have been since this old wreck had had a proper key? He shoved the ring-pull in the ignition lock and turned. A little red light came on. It worked! Now what? He'd seen loads of people kick-start bikes: how easy was it? He'd soon find out. He swung his leg over the saddle and sat astride the ageing mount. Then he kicked down hard - and sucked with pain as his foot shot off and the pedal skinned his calf. He hissed a swear-word. Then kicked again. Not hard enough.

"Oh God!" he snarled.

Any second now there'd be a whistle and a ruck and it would all be over.

"Please!"

And the dig would go on and the mound would be ravaged. Desecrated.

"Come *on*!"

He kicked again, and something fired.

"Yes!"

The engine was rumbling! But what now? Jo rummaged through his mind to find an image of what he'd seen Mort do: no picture came; but he turned both handlebars, pulled on a lever, kicked on something else and... the bike started moving. It was moving! Gears? He hadn't a clue. But as he fumbled and wrestled with handle and pedal something changed and he was moving faster. He opened what he thought was the throttle more and the noise was horrendous. But the bike was moving, and in a thunderous cloud of blue exhaust he steered his way to the mound and around the base.

What happened next was confusion. Total con-*fusion*.

A policeman dashed from the shadows and tried to grab him as he passed, but Jo shoved him off. Someone else jumped down from the mound into his path, but Jo swerved, hit a dustbin, swerved again and scraped with a sickening grate along a flash parked car, ripping off the wing mirror into the bargain; but he couldn't see a thing: no lights! So he pulled out his torch and flashed it all around - a wild attempt to signal rather than to light his way - and as he came below the dig-site into the glare of the arc-lamps he saw Annie, Richie, Don and Dave swearing and cursing that the plan was shot to pieces; and a trumpet blared and Jo was stirred from his slumping pose on the roof of the keep. He looked over the battlements and peered through the thin dawn light. And down below he saw Gareth and Morton riding into the bailey, their shining company of knights following behind; and the king, clad in Laurence's blue gown, marching across the snowy ground, arms outstretched in a gesture of welcome, and Gareth and Morton about to dismount. At any moment, he knew, the king's gesture would change and there would be slaughter. Why had he been so weak and delayed so long? He cried out:

"Gareth! Morton!"

He saw eyes look up and scan the sky. They couldn't see him. He waved, frantic - it made no difference. Ah! His torch! He pulled out his torch and flashed it wildly. But dawn was spreading, red and fierce, and the torch was a pin-prick in the brightening sky. Down below the knights were looking no longer, but stepping from their stirrups. Jo clambered on to the battlement, at the very spot from where Laurence had plunged, and waved and yelled with all the force he could muster:

"Gareth! It's the king!"

And Jo's dad came hurtling from the darkness, arms outstretched, and thrust both hands full into his chest.

"Morton! It's a trick!"

And Jo couldn't keep hold of the handlebars, and felt himself toppling from the saddle.

"The guards are all armed! They're going to trap you!"

An arrow was arcing through the air - Merlin must be silenced - and Jo saw it; and he fell backwards and crashed on to the sidecar; and far below Dagonet was crying: "To arms! To arms! It's treachery!"; and the bike hit a wall and flipped into the air, and Jo tried to duck to avoid the arrow, and he hit the ground and the motorbike smashed down on his legs, and Merlin was suddenly in air and falling.

11. The Vessel

*L*ying on a bed of gentle turf, the maiden close beside him. Jo awoke, and as he turned to look at her he sensed her softly smiling. All around was a deep, enfolding, womb-like darkness. It was very warm, and smelled of summer grass. It was strange to see her so close: the maiden murdered in the fountain, the maiden buried by the king. How did he come to be with her? And where were they? He lay and looked into her face. As he did so, it slowly struck him that he would never, later, be able to describe it. It was young and it was not young. It was of all time and of no time. It was there and it was not there. And he had always known it.

Eventually she said: "Do you hear it?"

Jo turned his head, and listened. He could hear a distant rumble.

"They are preparing," she said, gently. "They don't know what awaits them here."

Jo breathed, long and slow, and enjoyed the rise and fall. Then at last he asked: "What is this place?"

"The Mound," she said. "The Mother."

Jo considered this for a long while before saying: "I don't understand."

"Where else should I be?" the maiden answered slowly. "I am part of her, and in time shall *be* her. They freed me from the treasure-tower - they toppled it, destroyed it utterly - because of

144

you, your warning, just in time. Merlin fell like bird from bough, but your cry saved the shining company, the trap failed, and they had the victory. And they placed you here in your *esplumoir*, your moulting-place, that you might be renewed."

Jo just about understood, and said: "And you?"

"They placed me with you, Merlin, to await the time when I may be reawakened, if men have the will. But now they mean to violate this place: listen."

Jo listened again, and far, far above he could hear a moving engine. Excavation with a giant digger had begun.

"And if they do so," she whispered, "it will break them."

"I still don't really understand," said Jo. "If we're inside the mound, how did we come to be here?"

"The night the treasure-tower fell," the maiden said, "when all were sleeping, the hag appeared, the vessel in her hands; and rising tall on the ox's back she held the vessel high, and caught the moon's rays in its bowl and turned them on the Mother-mound in a dazzling beam; and through the white, white belly was cut a shaft through which you and I could be safely bedded in her womb. That shaft is what they intend to tear wide open."

Jo lay and pondered this for a long time. And when he turned his head to look at her again, it was his mother's eyes he was gazing at; and they were widening with wonder, and she said with a gasp that made her voice a whisper:

"Jo!" And then: "Nurse! Nurse! He's back!"

And a nurse appeared behind her, leaning over the bed in the hospital's white light.

"He's back!" his mother said again. "Jo! You're back! You're back!"

She was crying, smiling, radiant.

"Mum?" said Jo, uncertainly.

"Yes, I'm here, Jo," she said, and sat on the bed. "Don't worry now, I'm here."

He looked at her, completely baffled. Then:

"I did ring," he said, and thought back to the 'phone booth in the forest. "I did try."

His mother was silent.

"I thought you answered," he added, "but wouldn't speak to me."

His mother hung her head.

"Why wouldn't you talk to me, Mum?"

"I'm sorry, Jo," she said at last. "I was angry. I - I just - ". She stopped, and then, with bitterness but determination in her green-brown eyes, looked up and said: "I thought you were on your father's side."

"And I didn't want to leave a message on that stupid machine," said Jo, his eyes filling up. "I'd got nothing to say, really, because - well - I didn't think you'd understand."

"Understand what?"

"What's been happening."

"What *has* been happening, Jo?"

Jo tried to shift in bed, and gave a sharp cry of pain: his legs were agony.

"Don't move," the nurse said, leaning over him in a frumpish blue outfit and tucking his sheet tight behind his shoulders. "If it's very bad I'll get your painkillers: it's about time."

Jo nodded; and when the nurse had gone he wrestled a hand free and wiped his eyes and said: "What's happened to my legs, Mum?"

"That's the only thing I do know," she replied, and dabbled with her necklace of Indian beads as if it were a rosary. "You were riding a motorbike, for goodness' sake, and your father knocked you off and it fell on you. What it was all about I can't imagine."

"Am I going to be okay?"

Suddenly the conversation stopped. To Jo's horror his question was met with silence. His mum didn't reply. All he could do was stare at her.

"Mum - am I?"

Her eyes were fixed on the vinyl floor, and she was biting her lip.

"Am I? Will I...?" He stopped, barely able to ask the question. But he had to. "Will I be able to... play? Football?"

She wouldn't look up. There was another spell of awful silence. Jo tried to kick the blankets. But nothing happened.

He couldn't kick.

He closed his eyes and screwed them tight, and felt a welling cry of waste and desolation.

Then she said: "I don't think they're sure, Jo."

He heard these words and knew they were the kindest she could give him. He knew they meant much worse. Somehow he held the cry inside himself and opened his eyes again. They looked blankly at the ceiling.

Strip lights. Polystyrene tiles.

A wasteland.

He tried to fill the waste with goals - three tiles wide and one tile high - and saw balls curling into corners and flying in off post and crossbar. But the scorer was no longer him. It never would be now.

Minutes passed - it might have been two, it might have been ten - in which he was faintly aware of swallowing two tablets, and his mother asking what fruit he fancied, and if he'd like a book or two. Then a motorbike passed by outside. His mind made a dim connection, and:

"Did they catch them?" he said, flatly. "Or did they get away?"

"What? Who do you mean, Jo?"

"Gareth and - erm - the people who were trying to stop the dig."

His mother shook her head and frowned. "I've no idea, Jo."

Jo thought for a moment, and then said: "I think they got away. It's the only thing that makes sense."

"But your father's there now, of course," said his mother, and instantly her voice hardened and her mouth tensed. "Has he been to see you? No: all he can think about is his work - and money. He was going on about television rights: apparently there's a chance of amazing things preserved at the bottom of the mound."

"Yes," said Jo. "There are. And Mum?"

"What, love?" she said, her ringed fingers stroking his hair.

And as the tablets took effect and his eyes began to swim Jo said: "I think Dad's in terrible danger."

* * *

"It's coming," the maiden said, but lay quite still on the bed of turf; and Jo listened with her, intently, to the churning rumble up above. "Yes, it's coming," she said again. "The worst violation of all. The Mother-mound has been so abused: a castle keep; a winding path all lined with trees to deny her shape; a cistern and a chimney; her very presence masked on every side - how many even know the mound is here? - and now they mean to burrow in and ransack what they will not understand. They imagine a buried treasure here. They are right - but they will not recognise it."

She closed her eyes and breathed deeply; then she whispered:

"This mound is the Mother, the great goddess, the trinity of maiden-mother-hag who gives and who takes away. This is her womb, the vessel of life, and it needs to be held in reverence, not torn apart and plundered. The goddess now is dying of neglect. Her being - *life*'s being - depends on our devotion to her. Because she is denied respect, the earth is turned into a wasteland. They seek to build a treasure-tower by ravaging the sacred."

"Can't they be stopped?" asked Jo.

"Yes," she said, "but you will need to do it."

"Me? How?"

"Take this."

As they lay together, side by side in the warm darkness, she gently passed it across to him and laid it on his chest. It was the vessel - the open bowl with the dazzling light that had fed and warmed him in his prison cell, the vessel the hag had shown the waiting court.

"What use is it?" said Jo. "The hag said its light would be denied to all until it was held in reverence."

"And the wasteland would remain. You remember well."

"So what am I to do with it?"

"You'll see."

Then the maiden looked straight up, suddenly alert.

"Listen," she said. "They're arguing."

"I can't hear anything," said Jo.

"Yes you can. *Listen.*"

And Jo could hear it all, and picture it in his mind. Up above, someone warning, doubtful; and his father replying impatiently, insisting it was time. Then another voice - Dave? Annie? - alarmed, and then a chorus of yells, and a heaving crash.

"What was that?" said Jo.

"A tree," the maiden answered. "They are undermining the trees with their digging. One has just toppled, its roots ripping out the chalk. If they continue, they will destroy the mound entirely."

There was silence for a moment, then voices raised again, agitated, aggressive, hard.

"What's happening now?" said Jo.

"I would say," the maiden replied, listening, "that they've realised excavation is impossible. But your father is determined, Merlin, determined to penetrate this place. I'd say he was planning to come in."

"What do you mean?"

"I mean he's going to journey down the tunnel."

"Is it wide enough?"

"Oh yes," she said. "Wide and straight. As straight as the beam of light that made it. But he'll need to travel prostrate, lying on his belly."

Now came another noise: a light, rolling rumble.

"What's that?" said Jo.

"We'll know," the maiden answered, "soon enough."

If Jo and the maiden had been above, on the mound's side at the tunnel's mouth, they would have seen pictures on the monitor, relayed from the robot camera as it slipped and slid once more down the smooth, smooth chalk of the tunnel floor.

Only this time it was followed by a man. Jo's father was heaving and thrusting down the tunnel's walls, sliding ever nearer to his obsessive goal.

"He is fearless," said the maiden.

So absorbed were the archaeological team, their eyes fixed on the monitor, that they didn't see three figures slip quietly towards them down the mound's steep flank. They stopped some yards away, and knelt among the nettles, watching. They saw their motorbike and sidecar lying battered against a wall, but were more concerned with what would appear on the screen.

"He's mad," an engineer was saying. "Can he breathe down there? And how will he get back?"

"We've got a cord attached to his belly," said lanky Richie. "We can pull him out."

"What's he going to do when he gets there?"

"Dig," said Dave in his wheezing voice. "There's a pile of turf, all perfectly preserved. Whatever's underneath will be immaculate!"

"He's nearly here," the maiden whispered to Jo.

"He's nearly there!" said Annie, pointing to the screen. "Look, there it is again! The matted grass, and the flying ant!"

"I've got a confession to make," chuckled Richie. "The first time we saw that, I thought it was a beard!"

"Merlin's beard, right?" said Dave with a squeaky laugh.

"UBI NUNC SAPIENTIS OSSA MERLINI!" Annie intoned.

"Do what?" said Don.

"The town's motto: 'WHERE NOW ARE THE BONES OF WISE MERLIN'."

"Ooh, get you!"

"Make ready, Merlin," the maiden said. "He is almost here."

"Hey!" said Richie suddenly. "What's that?"

They all looked fixedly at the screen.

"It's a hand!" Annie was beaming. "His hand. He's reaching out, about to dig!"

"It is time," said the maiden, "for him to see."

"Come on, let's see it!" Dave said. "What's there?"

The screen showed groping fingers delve into the Stone Age grass - turf cut with the shoulder blade of an ox. And as he tore the turves apart, and trained the camera's light on what lay beneath -

"It's a bowl!" cried Annie.

"Superb!" said Dave.

- Jo's father was suddenly still and silent. He was staring at a face: a face he knew and didn't know at all: his son, was it? - how could it be? - or a being from another age, or deep within his mind?

And then he saw the vessel on his chest.

For heartbeat after heartbeat he was speechless, breathless, utterly wonder-struck. And then, very slowly, and barely able to form the words, he asked:

"What was it for? Who did it serve?"

Then he saw the other face, the maiden's face. And she was saying:

"You have asked the question, and you will have the answer. It served everyone, and it does so still, but unless it is held in reverence it will not do so forever. It is the vessel of life, the holy grail."

At hearing a voice beneath the earth, at the wonder of her final word, and at the shining vessel itself, Jo's father gaped like a little child. At last he whispered: "It's the most beautiful thing I've ever seen. And who," he asked, "are you?"

"I am the Maiden, the great goddess, the trinity of maiden-mother-hag who gives and who takes away. And you are hurting me. But Merlin understands."

"Merlin?" he said, looking at the face beside her. "Jo?"

"Dad," Jo said gently. "I think you should stop."

His father looked from one to the other, then back again, entirely bewildered; his world in a moment was turning upside-down: everything he'd ever believed, perceived, written or learnt, desired or valued was undone, evaporated; and this un-made man felt his face crumpling and tears starting in his eyes, and he said:

"Yes. Yes. I'm sorry."

And with that, the maiden changed before his eyes from girl to woman to ancient hag and then to woman again; and the last said:

"Turn the vessel, Merlin, to the light."

And as Jo turned it to face the camera, it caught the light's rays in its bowl and blazed them back in a dazzling beam; and the screen above turned a shattering white, the monitor blasting into shards; from deep inside the tunnel came a diabolic howl of pain, and Jo saw his father, only feet from him, cover his eyes too late from the vessel's blinding power.

"Get him out! Get him out!" Above, pandemonium; and Gareth, Mort and Dag looked on with pity as, gasping, frantic, the archaeologists heaved at the cord and hauled the wretched, blinded man from the tunnel's mouth. And as he slid from its lip and the tunnel was clear, an immense surge of light shot forth and blazed across the sky.

"Mum," said Jo, his eyes opening and widening.

"What is it, love?"

"My legs."

"What's happened?" said the nurse, hurrying to his bedside.

"They're really warm," Jo said. "I can move again. I really can."

On a battlemented city wall a breeze caught an array of banners: they hung limp no longer, but billowed, shining, in the wind; and King Arthur looked down upon this city and saw the streets a throng of life; and beyond the gates a river teemed with silver fish and stooping heron; and the fields were swaying with wheat and barley.

"The grail is found," he whispered.

Some outlaws, huddled round a winter fire, were startled, as all around the forest clearing, trees were bursting into leaf: brown was giving way to green; and their captain stood entranced as he saw Marian, free, alive, walking towards him through the melting snow.

"Time to go," said Gareth, and he nodded towards the motorbike below them at the mound's foot. Beside him Dag the nutter laughed, and standing up among the nettles he pointed and gurgled with derision at the body sprawled by the tunnel's mouth and the people staring at a shattered screen.

"Don't mock," said Mort. "Even I wouldn't do that."

"When his sight returns," Gareth pondered, "do you think he'll see?"

And Dag said: "I think they *all* will, now."

They scrambled down the mound and jumped on to the path beside the bike. They heaved it upright, and Dag hopped into the sidecar and Mort and Gareth swung into the saddle. No-one even noticed them as the ring-pull turned in the ignition, pedals and handles twisted and kicked, and the old machine went sputtering on its way.

* * *

"I'm sorry I'm so late getting it back."

The man at the bike hire didn't seem to mind. He wiped his stained hands on a greasy rag as he emerged from racks of wheels and tyres.

"That's okay, son," he said to Jo. "But where did you find to ride it? The whole countryside's been closed with the foot and mouth."

"Yeah. Yeah, I know, it was awful."

Jo didn't like to admit he'd only just collected the bike after days at the mercy of thieves and the elements. It was a miracle he could return it at all.

"Still, everything's open again!" the bikeman said. "Amazing, eh? The disease just vanished overnight. Thank God."

"Yes," said Jo. "Something like that."

"What?" The man blinked at the odd remark.

"It was a great bike!" Jo said with a beaming smile. "Thanks a lot! How much do I owe you?"

He loved the oily, rubbery smell of this place, with shining bikes and a thousand parts all stacked, hung and stashed in a toy-cupboard clutter. It was warm-hearted, childish, chaotic.

"Mmm, yeah, well. Glad you enjoyed it," said the bikeman, shy and embarrassed, unused as he was to such effusiveness about his humble dealings; and as he gave the price and took the money from Jo he said: "I tell you what. You've had more than a week so you get a free day. Do you want it?"

Jo thought about this for a moment, jingling the change in his hand. Then he grinned and said:

"You're very kind. Thanks a lot. That would be great."

His mum was bringing Kate to see him at six. He couldn't wait. But there was the whole afternoon to enjoy before then. He knew where he wanted to go.

* * *

There was nothing between him and the brilliant August sun. He was level with every surrounding hill. And in the bowl of fields below him, sheep and cattle grazed and drank, and barley, dusky gold, was being harvested with a timeless satisfaction.

There on the top of Silbury Hill - the great sister of the hidden, tree-masked, cistern-and-chimneyed Merlin mound - he felt at the centre of all things.

He jogged around its grassy top: he could run again. He ran faster and faster, round and round in mazy circles till his head spun,

154

and was just about to fling himself into the grass when a voice, far down below, yelled:

"Hoy! You're not supposed to be up there!"

Jo stood still, panting. Then he bent down, picked up his football, and with his right foot launched it high into the sky.

ALL THE LOCATIONS in this story are real, as are the facts about them. In particular, the mound of the title is the colossal Stone Age mound - complete with eighteenth-century grotto - almost entirely hidden among the buildings of the college at the western end of Marlborough High Street. It is the legendary burial place of Merlin, but dates from the same period as the world-famous Silbury Hill a few miles further along the A4 near Avebury, and was used in the Middle Ages as the motte of a great castle especially favoured by King John. As is the way with things, of course, some of the places have changed during the book's writing: a hotel bar is now a branch of a pizza chain, a building site is now a building, and Silbury is currently crowned with a fence guarding an enormous hole, the result of crude archaeology.

THE STORY would never have taken shape had I not read Michael Dames's inspirational books *The Silbury Treasure* and *The Avebury Cycle* (reissued by Thames & Hudson in paperback editions in 1992 and 1996); also *Symbolic Landscapes* by Paul Devereux (Gothic Image, 1992) and *Legendary Landscapes* by J.D.Wakefield (Nod Press, 1999). All are highly readable and warmly recommended. The book referred to by Laurence and King John is Robert de Boron's *Merlin and the Grail*, a late twelfth century work which also explains more about the vessel and Merlin's birth. It is available in a translation published by Boydell & Brewer in 2003. The song sung by Gareth and Mort is the chorus of *The Motorcycle Song* by Arlo Guthrie, recorded on his album *Alice's Restaurant*.